Charley
through
Canada

Carolyn R. Parsons

Rose Enna Imprints

Rose Enna Imprints

ISBN:0986500631

ISBN-13:978-0986500633

DEDICATION

For my Family
Who have had to put up with my obsession with making stuff
up.
**My husband, Kent, as well as Alyssa, Scott, Ethan, Chayce,
Dante, Aleena, Christie, Curtis, Dominic, Sophia &
Martina**
I adore you all

And for Mom, Brian, Fred & Elizabeth.
Who support our family in too many ways to mention

And especially for Uncle Bruce and Aunt Bonnie Parsons
For their hospitality, their kindness, and the example they set
every single day
on how to live a good and generous life.
Lessons on being a family, on how to love, how to give and how
to share,
were taught to me last summer, likely, without you even realizing
you were teaching them.
My gratitude forever
Thank you.

ACKNOWLEDGMENTS

It is with appreciation I thank all who made this book possible. Thank you to my writer friends Kate Sparkes & Candace Osmond who are new in my life but already make me feel like this strange world of make-believe is as important as the strange real world, as well as a reflection of it. Special thanks to my long-time writer friend, Lia Mack, who inspires, supports and understands. Thank you to Corey Majeau, graphic designer, who grabbed hold of a last-minute project and made a vision into reality. To the Romancing the Rock Group, much gratitude for your amazing talent that raises the bar for all . Thank you especially to the country that inspired this book, one that allowed me the peace and the freedom to pursue my dreams, and offers the same gift to all who inhabit its vast lands. Thank you to Canadians, who make this country all it is.
And most important of all, thank you to the readers. I appreciate you taking your precious time to spend it reading my stories. It is truly humbling and the most gratifying part of my work.

Chapter 1

What is yesterday but a time when people forget to enjoy life before it exists and bask in after its realization. Where minds and souls and psyches go for protection from the pain of the present. Or avoid, due to trauma found there. Charlotte Andrews was a yesterday-avoider. Glory days and gory days are both found in yesterdays. It was the gory ones Charley avoided. There were precious few glory days.

On Friday, the 2016 Ford Edge shone like brand new. Its frosted red paint gleamed after a short drive through a thick stream of rainbow soap and high gloss wax. That was the day before though. *Yesterday*. Today the sun hid, its rays tempered by the fat clouds that drifted across the sky. Seconds later rain sprinkled the lush greenery of the island. Within moments it fell in a steady stream. The people who milled around, chatting and waiting, hopped into their vehicles to avoid the impending downfall.

The first raindrops hit the windshield in big splats. The droplets' pit-pat, pit-pat percussion increased in tempo. Wayward streams ran down the windshield, spreading to the left and right, following invisible trails blazed by the effects of some magical concoction the car wash used.

Nope. She never spent time thinking about yesterday. She put each one behind her as soon as it was done. Work complete. Time filled. Lessons learned. Car wash ruined. So, what? Another day lived. That was all it was. Another ordinary day. Survived. Done. Check. Move on.

It would have been a perfect way to live except Charlotte Andrews hated being ordinary. Somehow though, ordinary had sneaked upon her as sure as the tide creeps upon the shores from one moon to another, rising, enveloping her over time. As a young woman, it didn't seem possible it would be so. Audacious and confident, poised to do something amazing, she had been a natural leader. Charlotte had been ready to make her mark, bound to impress the world.

The reasons she spent fifteen years becoming ordinary on Canada's west coast, while plentiful and understandable, dissipated over time. The tick of the clock, the flip of the calendar distanced her from those reasons until they had morphed into mere excuses. Out from underneath common and average, peeked a new woman. It was tenuous, she was nervous, but now in her early forties, ambition, drive and energy renewed, Charlotte was ready for another go at life.

Known only as Charley to the followers on Facebook and her blog, *Through Canada,* she sat in the red Ford. Pen scribbling, lips curled to the left in concentration, she wrote in her spiral-bound note book as she put her thoughts about the trip on paper. Exploring the country, making her way eastward to where her Grandmother lived in Change Islands, Newfoundland, why, the idea was inspired. Going island to island, coast to coast, through a country she loved, well, it had a certain romantic element to it, right?

It was, in many ways, a business trip. After all, it would be shared with her readers. She had built up a following on her Facebook fan page and had a healthy Twitter and Instagram following as well. Interest had peaked in the days before she set off and her promise to live-stream portions of the trip were met with enthusiasm. She didn't quite know why she had become so popular but her regular, short, entries and her knack for social media promotion, along with a few well-placed ads, had worked.

The Tragically Hip blasted from her speakers as she re-read her first entry, her face scrunched into a grimace.

"July 1

Perhaps through the individual determination that a nation cannot be defined, we learn to understand it more . To even attempt to reconcile the idea of Canada to the reality of it is a naive and foolish endeavor. I embark upon it anyway. Perhaps I am a fool? Over these past one hundred and fifty years a nation has been created that has become a beacon of hope. Canada has evolved into a country recognized as a standard-bearer of democracy and peace. But living in it, one easily forgets. I am surrounded by people who are flawed, inadequate, whiny, apathetic and above all, entitled.

I am one of them. What is so special about being that?

But, if I think about it more, I am also surrounded by giving, caring, thoughtful and selfless people. Not that there is any sacrifice there, in a country with so much. I am one of them too.

It is no big gift to give, if you have plenty. To have little and offer, is far greater sacrifice.

The privilege of peace is a veil through which I watch life unfold. Behind the shroud my own personal experience has transpired. My unique pain is something I never set free upon the world, because it does not serve to ruin the mirage. I wonder if I'm the only one."

She shook her head.

"That is the lamest, corniest thing I've ever written in my God-damned life," she said out loud, closing notebook over pen, setting both on the passenger seat. She pulled her baseball hat forward and frowned at the buzz of the telephone.

"Nan. Jesus, not again." She tapped the Bluetooth button. Her grandmother's relentlessness in her pursuit of this *favour* was driving her crazy. "Hi Nan, I know why you're calling." She had promised an answer this morning.

"I always say you cannot do a kindness too soon, for you never know how soon it'll be too late." Orla Andrews held the phone tucked between her jaw and neck, hands busy slicing apples.

"Grandmother, *you* didn't say that, *Ralph Waldo Emerson* did."

"Whatever. And don't '*grandmother*' me young lady. This Emerson feller was right which is why I always say it. The young man needs a ride and that's that. We don't leave people stranded. He'll be at the ferry when you get off, or somewhere in Vancouver ."

"Jesus. Nan, What if he's a serial killer or something? Have you even thought of my safety here?" She had made this argument before. It was pointless. "Plus, this is a working thing and my dream vacation all rolled in one and I am used to being alone. I like being alone. I don't even have a cat, Nan."

Charley pulled the pony tail that weaved through the opening at the back of her baseball hat tight by grabbing half in each hand and yanking.

The pain at the tug helped her forget a fear that niggled elsewhere.

"He is safe. I wouldn't send my favourite granddaughter on a trip with a serial killer. You need to get over suspecting everybody. He's a nice man. Ger wouldn't have suggested, neither would I if he wasn't. He was a Mountie for crying out loud. I daresay you're safer with him than by yourself. Ger says he's a quiet feller, he doesn't have much luggage and you're coming this way."

"I'm your *only* Granddaughter. Jeez. Does he know it could take me up to a month to get home, I'm not coming straight across. I have a plan." She didn't. She had ideas and options but no real plan. But that was part of her objection, she didn't want to have plans. She had booked her first accommodations—only because it was Canada Day. Between then and the Marine Atlantic ferry reservation in a few weeks, she had one goal. To see as much of the country as she could.

"I still don't understand why he can't fly."

"He can't. You're going to have to trust me on that. If he tells you why along the way that's up to him but I'm sworn to secrecy."

"Don't you think that's a bit friggin' weird? That he's unable to fly? Afraid to fly?"

"It's not, now look..." Orla began before Charlie cut her off.

"Nan, I have to go, we're loading. I can't talk while we're loading." She put the car into drive and pulled forward, flicking on the wipers. The marshall area was full. It was a busy time being both the weekend and Canada Day. Most people were coming to Bowen Island for the day, not leaving like Charley. But her line was still full.

"You'll pick him up? Ger needs to know. He's her only grandson you know and she worries." Her voice with its soft lilt filled the van. Orla Andrews knew she had won.

"Yes, I s'pose I must, tell Ger yes. I gotta go Nan. I'll talk to you after I'm across. I love you, bye."

She moved along further, smiling at the deckhand as she drove onto the ferry. The air was still, the rain was coming straight down. She tapped off the Bluetooth and hit the button for her window.

"Thank you!" she said with a bright smile.

"You have a nice trip," he replied with a grin and a wave. In her years on the island on British Columbia's far west coast, teaching at Bowen Island Community School, she had chatted to many of the ferry workers on the twenty-minute cruise on the one hundred car ferry that connected the island to Horseshoe Bay on the mainland.

Once parked on board, she made her way to the Coast Cafe Express to grab a coffee. Like many who shared the trip with her she was wearing red and white in honour of Canada Day. Unlike most, she had a suitcase full of similar T-shirt & Tank tops with a logo that said *Charley through Canada*.

She sipped her coffee, looking back for a moment, something she didn't often do, preferring to keep her nose, always, pointed straight forward. The wake of the ferry rolled until it washed the dock, back in Snug Cove. Never did one of these tiny alcoves of land have a more apt moniker. Comfortable, warm and cozy. Well-protected from the weather. How safe it made her feel to pull into the port with its comforting name. To come home. This island, a place to call hers, a sanctuary, where nobody truly knew her, no matter how long she stayed.

Now she had to deal with what's-his-name. What *was* his name again? Damn. She sipped her coffee, adjusted her sun glasses but put them back on her hat again, they were spotted with droplets. Garry. That was it. He grew up in Twillingate or New World Island or somewhere *'longside* as Nan put it. Geraldine Clarke had asked that Charley drive her grandson. Nan had implored until Charley agreed. So, there it was. She was stuck. She didn't like it at all. Making small talk across Canada was not part of her plan. What if he was a grouchy, negative, arrogant, complaining, blowhard?

She'd drop him off at a truck stop and let him hitchhike home, that's what.

The Queen of Capilano's engines quietened as they entered Horseshoe Bay. Charley walked to her vehicle, coffee in hand, determined this man, this Garrison, would not ruin her trip.

"Sometimes you wanna go where everybody knows your name," she sang the *Cheers* theme song under her breath, her thoughts turning to a tiny island far across the country where everybody did know her name.

A thought from the past snuck in and the song died on her lips. She gave her head a tiny shake.

"Not thinking of that," Charley said out loud, slipping into her car. It was all many yesterdays ago.

Chapter 2

The wipers swatted at the incessant rain, the blades scraping as fast as they could. When it let up for a moment she reduced the speed but then, it rained harder. In some places the wind gusts, in Vancouver the rain does. Charley was once more on the phone with her grandmother.

"Nan, I know where I'm going. I won't get lost. I live here for crying out loud. I'll find the place. Look I have to go okay?" Charley said in her third attempt to end the call.

"Ger said you needs to be patient with him," Orla Andrews advised.

Charley's patience had been a slippery thing to start with and now it slid away for good.

"Nan, this is nuts. Am I picking up a grown man or a kid? Look, if he doesn't behave he's getting dropped off at a truck stop! Remember I'm doing him the favour. This is my trip, my vacation. Now I know you think it's a big waste of time and money and I just should have flown but I have been planning and saving for this trip for forever and I'm not ruining it because this guy is a fragile butterfly and needs patience. Perhaps he needs to be patient with me." She held back the *for fuck sakes* that wanted to punctuate the sentence.

"I knows you don't like men, and God knows you got your reasons but that's no excuse for getting saucy with me missy," Orla snapped back. But without real anger. Her granddaughter was right.

"Look Nan, I'm driving the guy. I'm sorry but he's going to have to behave. I'm not changing a thing or doing one thing different than I planned. I should go, I'm coming up on my exit now. Plus, it's raining sheets here and I can't concentrate when the phone is on. I'll call you after."

She tapped the Bluetooth button on the dash of her car and Nan was gone. She ignored the twinge of guilt. Orla was a handful but her heart was golden. Plus, she was no basket of peaches herself. This guy Garry might decide he couldn't tolerate her and hop out and hitchhike before they hit the Alberta border. She could only hope.

The service station came into sight and Charley pulled in and drove up to one of the gas bays. She paid at the pump and when she was done, moved into a parking spot. She slipped out and headed to the bathroom, something she could have delayed for an hour if she didn't have this guy waiting.

By now all the pertinent information would have been relayed to Geraldine who would call her grandson Garry and describe what to look for. A red Ford Edge, British Columbia License Plate CHAR*ANN, Canadian Flag flying on the antenna, vinyl decal on the rear side window with a big Red maple leaf that said *Charley through Canada*, the driver a slender brunette, five-foot-eight, with brown eyes, wearing a t-shirt that matched the window graphic.

He'd find her easy enough so Charley didn't look for him. If he didn't show up by the time she peed, grabbed a Timmie's and was ready to hit the road it was his loss. Perhaps he would decide to take a faster route and find a lonely truck driver who would get him across the country more quickly. *If she was lucky*. She exited the Tim Horton's and her hopes were dashed.

Jesus, he's tall, she thought. He was well over six-feet. He sported a pair of black rimmed glasses, his wet, dark curly hair past his ears.

"So, you like your Timmie's too do you?" she said, eyeing the two brown cups in his hands. She had two in hers as well, "come on, we have to get in fast."

It still rained a little. She clicked her key fob by pressing it against one cup to open the doors.

"Can't do without my double-double. I'm Garry and you're Charley?"

So, he wasn't a complete grouch, nice smile and eyes. Ordinary. And he'd bought her coffee.

Her nod was barely noticeable, "Nan says you need a ride. Hang on, I've got tons of space in the car."

She put the cups in the front cup holders and he set his two in the back-seat holders at her suggestion. She grabbed the umbrella left behind when the rain lulled & went around to the back. She reached out from under her umbrella as the trunk-lid opened. She shook his hand. It was warm, his grasp firm.

"It is nice to meet you; the lid is open for your bags," she stated the obvious.

Before he could do anything Charley had an impish impulse. She'd test his patience, see if his sense of humour was intact or if she was transporting some sort of fuddy-duddy across the country. She looked deep into his eyes and stood upon her toes, her nose in the air. She could tell he was holding his breath as she moved closer. About an inch from his face she moved hers to the left and inhaled, a great, loud, exaggerated sniff. She sniffed the other side, making a great show of it.

"What the hell are you doing?" He tripped trying to move away.

"I'm smelling you. I must make sure you don't stink. You see my Nan, Orla Andrews, tells me last night there is this guy who wants to drive across Canada with me and I told her yes but with one condition. I can tolerate anything, I'm pretty easy going but I can't deal with somebody who stinks. That includes smoking so if you smoke you'll have to make it clear across the country without a draw. You don't smell like you smoke though and you've showered and you're clean. I think you pass the sniff test." She nodded, smiled and stepped back.

He laughed out loud, a great rolling sound.

"Do I get to sniff you back?" He leaned in.

"Sure, and if you decide I stink too badly you can hitchhike." She shrugged, a dare in her eyes. If only she had thought ahead. She could have hidden a couple fresh fish under his seat. In a few days, he'd be walking.

"Fair enough, I'm at your mercy. And no, I don't smoke. Never have." His laugh tapered back into a smile. His grandmother was right. She was funny. And nice.

Ice broken, they closed the hatch moments later, his bags tucked nicely in on top of hers. One suitcase, a garment bag and what appeared to be a guitar case on top of it all. The back went down slowly as they walked to the front of the car. He placed his back pack in the back seat.

"Nice vehicle," he commented as they climbed in, "I've always been a Ford guy."

"Thanks, I bought it last year specifically for this trip. It's a comfortable drive."

"My grandmother says you're going to take a month to get to Newfoundland? Are you stopping somewhere on the way?"

"I'm stopping everywhere. Didn't she explain about this trip?"

"She told me she had a ride for me with a nice teacher if I didn't mind taking up to a month to get home and you would pick me up here. She didn't want me to hitchhike."

"Well it's not the best way to travel so I can't blame her. But this is a promo-trip, a work trip, sort of." It was also an adventure, a rebirth but she didn't tell him that bit.

"No, hitchhiking is not ideal, but after my car died its final death, I though at least it would get me home. I'm in no hurry. However now I feel like I am intruding." Damn his grandmother. She was a darling but she worried about him too much. She had her reasons but still, he hated being an inconvenience.

"Why not fly? You could be home for the summer and that's the best time in Newfoundland," she ignored his comment, didn't want to lie, didn't want to tell the truth. Yes, he was intruding.

"Long story," he evaded, "and I'll have lots of summers in Newfoundland. This is a permanent move."

"Really? You didn't bring much with you."

It grew quiet. She glanced at him. He looked straight ahead.

"No. I don't own many things."

She nodded. "I own too many things. I think of shedding it all sometimes." There was a freedom that appealed in having less and she envied him, for a second. Not her books. She couldn't ever part with them. Or the gifts the kids gave her. Or her house. She loved the house.

"Yeah, that's what I did, I shed it all."

"Well bully for you." She strapped her seatbelt and he did the same and flipped open the plastic flap on his cup.

She put the Edge in gear and eased out, making her way across the parking lot, merging eastward into traffic.

"Canada here I, er, we come," she said, looking at her passenger who returned her smile and sipped his double-double, eyes rolling in exaggerated pleasure.

Regular double-double, Charley mused, tasting her dark roast. So, boring, cliché, ordinary. This trip isn't supposed to be ordinary, it is supposed to be fun and yes, work, but more than that. It is supposed to be about me, striking out on my own, getting to know myself, trying my refurbished, re-feathered wings, the phoenix resurrected from the ashes and stuff like that. Everything tied up with a Canadian bow.

Another thought perked her up a bit. A Mountie drinking Timmie's would be a great topic for her next blog post. It *was* super cliché but so Canadian. She peeked at him again. He had a tablet and was reading, his coffee still in his hand.

He switched to sunglasses and didn't look quite so nerdy. She pulled her attention back to the road. She needed to ignore him if this was going to work out. She started writing her next blog post in her head as she settled in at exactly the speed limit and set the cruise.

A Mountie with a Tim Horton's. Yep. It was an inconvenience but not a bad start to a Canadian adventure.

Chapter 3

Charley hit the entertainment button on the screen. Nights of sitting with her laptop, quite a few dollars spent on downloads and she had assembled the perfect play list. She hit shuffle and adjusted the volume.

"If you don't mind me asking, why exactly is this trip going to take an entire month? You want to see the country?" Garry interjected into her thoughts shortly after they were out in traffic and moving.

Charley withheld a sigh. So, they were going to talk.

"I'm not just out to see Canada. I'm out to discover it." She sipped her coffee.

"Isn't that pretty much the same thing?" Garry turned, staring at her profile.

"Not really. I'm trying to get a better understanding of what it means to be Canadian, you know, what is this...*Canada thing*. Let's face it, we've got something special going on here in this country, or so we're supposed to believe. So, what makes us a nation beyond our politics? I've lived on both coasts, but I've not been anywhere else for any amount of time. Yet I feel Canadian in my bones and my blog has tapped into that feeling in others. I think I am about as patriotic to this country as possible and yet, I haven't seen or been in the vast majority of it. So, I decided to set out to see if there is a Canada *feeling* or if I am brainwashed by the television and media and music to think Canada is an identifiable something. I don't know if that makes any sense to you." This explained the work part of the journey. The personal part was far more complex.

"Well, I've never given it much thought before but I am a Mountie. *Was* a Mountie. Can't get much more Canadian than that, can you? We're kind of an emblem, an identifiable Canadian symbol. So yeah, I'm patriotic and Canadian but I never gave much thought as to why. My mother was very patriotic. She drilled it into us. She was the ultimate Canadian. I'm not sure I would have gone out to discover it on purpose like this but I think this is great. Where do we go first?"

"We are going east." She shot him a look, surprised, and a bit flattered by his eagerness.

" Okay, so a surprise?"

"Yeah, for the most part. I want to immerse in it you know? Do some things, talk to Canadians, explore some of the tourist things but also explore some off-the-beaten path stuff. There is a bit of a plan. For example, I've got hundreds of songs on this play list. All Canadian. Alanis, Blue Rodeo, The Hip, KD Lang, Justin Bieber, hey don't give me that look, the kid is fantastic." She thought about her Stuart McLean collection also. His passing had been a sad moment for her and the country who loved his stories and it seemed appropriate to bring them along.

"He's a little shit," Garry said.

"What?" Oh, my God, the guy was a complete asshole. Stuart McLean was a Canadian icon, a treasure, an immeasurable loss for the— wait, she did spend too much time alone, in her own head. She hadn't said that out loud.

"Oh, Justin Bieber? Yeah well you were probably a little shit at twenty-two, twenty-three or whatever he is now. Still a baby. Hell, I can be a little shit on occasion. I just don't have the entire world watching."

Maybe a hundred thousand or so on a Facebook page. But they didn't see the *real* Charley.

"True enough I suppose." He hadn't ever given much thought to Justin Bieber. Just a kid who sang pop music.

"He's great and he wrote the ultimate Canadian song, *Sorry*." She laughed when he groaned.

"So, you're doing Canadian immersion, yet on Canada Day instead of fireworks and fun you're off on a road trip?" he asked, curiosity unsatisfied.

"What better day to start a Canadian adventure but on Canada day?"

"It's a bit lame, isn't it? No, no, I'm kidding…" The look she shot him had him scrunched against the door in mock horror. "I actually like this idea. This could be fun. Don't kill me, or worse, make me walk. Hey, do you mind if I take notes along the way? Record things, thoughts, ideas. I'll type them up for you after if you like, that way you have a record of the trip."

"Go for it. And it's obvious to me your grandmother didn't tell you about *Charley through Canada*?"

"Uh? Is that a thing? I mean other than the fact you're Charley and you're going through Canada?"

"Yes, it's a thing. I host a successful blog about Canada and have a lot of followers on Twitter and Facebook and Instagram. This trip is an extension of that called *Charley through Canada*. I do it for fun, in my spare time but it's caught on. I make a little money through some ads, and thought I'd use that to ramp it up a bit, take this trip. So, you're not going to interfere or get impatient when I veer off into a place I didn't plan to go because the whim strikes? Because that's how it's going to be. I'm also doing some Facebook Live things, maybe every day, reporting my adventures and so on."

"Wow? Are you famous? How many followers?" He pulled out his phone and started a search for her.

"A few thousand," she evaded, "and no, Charley is but Charlotte isn't. I use the alternative version of my first name and never say where I live. So far nobody knows who I am. Except Nan, and your grandmother, and everybody they've told down there. Maybe you can join me on one of the broadcasts? Oh, one more thing. Sometimes I like it quiet. Don't take it personally if I stop talking to you and go off in my own little world."

"I'll take a pass on the broadcast. Keep me out of it. Keep me anonymous too. Don't say anything that can identify me please. And if you don't go veering off the road into a ditch I'll leave you to your silence. I have my Kindle. I can read. I think I'll download some books about Canada when we get near some WIFI."

"Okay, deal on the anonymity." Too bad, it was a good idea. "Can I at least say you're a Mountie and yeah, I completely understand."

"Deal." He *liked* her *Through Canada* Facebook page, then swapped the phone for the Kindle, and lost himself in his book occasionally swiping his finger along the screen with a flip to turn the page of *The Illegals* by Laurence Hill.

Justin Beiber's voice broke into Charley's thoughts, the pop strains were fun driving music. She upped the volume a tad.

If you like the way you look that much, then you should go and love yourself.

She glanced at Garry and laughed out loud as she noted him singing the words, barely audible as he read.

"What?" He feigned innocence.

"You know the words. Who's the little shit?" She shook her head, amused as he did some seated Justin Bieber moves, pulling the visor down and admiring himself in the mirror, pantomiming loving himself.

He grinned, singing louder. Charley joined in.

"And I didn't wanna write a song 'cause I didn't want anyone thinking I still care but I don't but you still hit my phone up and baby I be movin' on and I think you should be somethin' I don't wanna hold back, maybe you should know that My Mama don't like you and she likes everyone, And I never like to admit that I was wrong...." They were both decent singers.

Well what do you know she thought, when the song and the laughs ended and she was driving along again to some Jann Arden. A Mountie with a sense of humour.

She was still wary but since she was stuck with him she might as well make the best of it. When Bryan Adam's gravelly voice started with *Cuts Like a Knife* they both sang along, giving each other sideways glances as she pulled out and passed a slow-moving RV. At least they agreed on the tunes.

Chapter 4

The rain stopped before they got to Alberta. A warm breeze blew from the west and the hot orange sun heated the mountains set against the bright blue sky.

"Blue Rodeo or Tragically Hip?" They stopped to pee and she was pumping gas when he returned from using the facilities.

"What? You're asking me?" He placed his hand over his forehead, palm out in mock surprise, winked, then pried open his coke, taking a swig.

"I want your opinion, I may not go with it." The pump clicked off and she pulled her card out to swipe it.

The van had been tided, their cups tossed in the garbage and he had thrown some bags of chips in the back seat. An ice-cold Dr. Pepper was in the driver side cup holder. He had earned a say.

"They're both pretty cool."

"Blue Rodeo it is."

"Five Days in July? I love that album. You know, I've only been to Jasper. Um, maybe we could go to Banff too? Can we do that?" Garry asked.

"Yeah I have that album and maybe we can do that. Google, it, check the route.

"You didn't plan anything, did you?"

"I booked a room at a hostel in Jasper for the night. Oh, you need to book yours. You're cute but you're getting your own room. I figured Canada Day might be busy. Plus, it's a Saturday. So, good luck. I don't think we'll have trouble getting a room the rest of the trip. I didn't book tomorrow night. But we can plan from here on in. Should be fine."

"You think I'm cute?" His eyebrows raised, fingers halting mid room-booking.

"Book your room please. Yeah, you're cute, do you have hiking boots?" He was a tall, nerdy, cute Mountie. No denying it.

"Yeah, I do. In the bigger bag. You're a hiker?"

"Crazy hiker. I am out every spare moment on the trails."

"Alone?"

"Yeah, I was thinking of joining a hiking group but never got around to it." Charley preferred it that way. She just couldn't deal with people much of the time so she found reasons not to.

"I like hiking in a group, I don't like it alone so much. I like to have company. I can't believe you think I'm cute. I'm not used to being cute though. Can't I be handsome, rugged, manly? Instead of merely cute?"

"I prefer to be alone and you're *just* cute. Accept it sunshine. We'll have to see how you handle yourself in the woods before I can apply any further adjectives."

"I will stay back if you prefer to be alone. I don't want to intrude." Ignoring her teasing, it was the first part of her statement he responded to. She might not want his company.

"Nah. We won't be the only ones out there on a trail in Jasper on Canada Day."

"True. Okay, I'm in. These mountains are incredible uh?" He nodded at the majestic, snow-capped peaks.

"Nope, lots of people around and yeah, beautiful."

"So, about this cute thing. What if I take down a beaver with my bare hands in my rugged, handsome, manly way. A Mountie wrestling a beaver. Think about it. That's Canadian. And masculine. Will I be more than cute then?"

The visual of this Mountie and a beaver wrestling formed in her mind and a laugh burst from her.

"You're a funny guy, and tolerable, but barely." She shook her head, an amused wryness in her voice.

"Cute *and* funny, I like those two, I'll focus on the positive and that's progress. Come on, let's go, I've things to prove. Here beaver, beaver, beaver!" He tapped the screen on his phone.

She shook her head, as he booked his room.

"So, what do you know about Jasper?" He finished his call and turned to her again.

"He's a character in *Twilight*."

"What?" his face furrowed, little lines crinkling his forehead.

"Never mind, I watch a lot of movies. Even bad ones. And speaking of bad ones, what do you think of Canadian movies. I need material for the blog." Might as well pick his brain since he was here and she was stuck for a topic.

"I think they are," he hesitated, "improving."

"Yeah they are. I'm going to admit something that must never leave this van." Her eyes darted around, furtive, as though there were listening devices everywhere.

"You have my word." He stuck up his fingers in a Boy Scout promise.

"I never liked Canadian movies," she confessed her shame, "and they always end funny. Don't you think they always end funny?"

"So we're under the dome here? We're in the Vegas of automobiles, nothing we say in the van, leaves the van? Right?" He tapped the window.

She looked in his direction for a moment, nodded, face solemn.

"Okay, then, yeah, I admit it. I'm a bad Canadian because I agree. And there's more. I have even come up with a theory on it." He tapped the window again, once more as if testing its sound-proof-ness.

"All clear, what is it?"

"Alright, here goes. Maybe I'm way off base and I'm sure there were good ones and maybe they were great artistic masterpieces of incredible brilliance I'm too simple-minded to comprehend or maybe we were spoiled by the great American movie industry with their big budgets and their happy fantasy endings, but," he took a breath, "my opinion is Canadian movie-makers were trying harder to say something, than to entertain, and sometimes it was over-the-top too clever. They wanted to impress movie-makers, not viewers. And well, clever doesn't appeal to the masses. I watch movies to escape, to learn. yes but mainly to escape. What is one movie you remember? You know, a quintessentially Canadian movie, that pops in mind?"

"Dome still secure?" At his nod, she continued, "*The Rowdyman.* Perhaps I choose that because I'm a Newfoundlander. A Nova Scotian probably has a different idea. Plus, it's the only one I can think of, off hand. Pinsent is a brilliant actor."

"That's a good example. You hear the title, *The Rowdyman* and you think, Canadian right?"

"Because it was God-awful and ends funny?"

"Was it god-awful?" It had been so long ago since he'd seen it.

"I thought it was. But I was young when I first saw it. There are people who love it but me, not so fussy about it. Why do we even think about that as a *great* Canadian movie?"

"Nostalgia? But nobody ever says so, right? People talk about it with reverence, like it's some sort of work of art." He couldn't remember liking it. Or watching it a second time.

"Perhaps it's the same as how nobody is supposed to say they don't care for some of Margaret Atwood's books. Because *she's* Margaret Atwood and well, she's *the* Canadian author. Now I'm in big trouble."

"Still secure chief, and I confess that I hated Oryx and Crake."

"Oh my God, me too, and with a passion that burns. I thought it was contrived and silly. And the names of the characters were so stupid. Did it have a plot? I don't remember. Some sort of dystopian disaster. But, now, *The Handmaid's Tale,* I read that when I was young and found it to be intense and thought-provoking but I had a teacher who despised the writing and concluded that by having it written by the character, Offred, Atwood could get away with awful writing because it wasn't *her* writing, it was the character's writing."

"That's an interesting take on *The Handmaid's Tale*. But I think that's a sign it's good, if it leaves you wondering. I like dystopian stories. Like I used to think about how to survive after a big flood, like in the Bible."

"I do too. For me it was more *Brave New World* though. This conversation has taken a weird turn," Charley said, but she was enjoying it.

"I think I'll write a book about how to survive a nuclear holocaust that destroys all but two people who are hiking in Jasper National Park and now must re-populate the human species..." Garry joked.

"The Handmaid's Tale was successful and that makes it good. And I haven't written any best-selling fiction books so who am I to judge? Oh and absolutely zero re-population from me. I'm too old plus humans are highly over-rated, we should leave the earth to the animals." Her heart thumped in her chest from--fright? Excitement? He was flirting? What the hell!

"I am reading Laurence Hill, he's my favourite Canadian author and we do have good movies. Ever hear of Jesus of Montreal?" Garry asked, looking at his phone and returning to their original discussion.

"Nope. What is it?" She was a bit disappointed the flirting had stopped. If that's what it was.

"One of the top ten Canadian films of all time according to the Toronto International Film Festival. I've never heard of any of these films. Ataparjuat: The Fast runner." He struggled over the pronunciation. "Mon Oncle Antoine, The Sweet Hereafter, Jesus of Montreal," Garry read the entire list through.

"So, the problem isn't maybe that we have some bad films, but that we don't see the ones that are good?"

"I think that might be it. Perhaps a distribution problem. We have to look too hard for them. Especially if we're not in the cities. When did you last see a Canadian film in the theater?"

"Other than the Justin Bieber, *Never Say Never*?"

"You and the Beebs! I don't think that's a Canadian film, just a film about a Canadian. But the dome can come up now because I personally think Canadians are more than excellent at documentary."

"I agree, absolutely, we tell in-depth, brilliantly-written investigative stories well in film. And television. Canadian television productions have improved so much. And we're funny. Mark

Critch? Rick Mercer? You can't argue their talent. So, you speak French?" She'd noticed his pronunciation of the French film titles.

"Oui." Garry was bilingual.

"Woohoo! Quebec is going to be fun."

"You want to learn some, we can practice on the way, this exit." Garry guided her to where she needed to turn to get to the town.

Early in the afternoon they checked into the Jasper Downtown Hostel. "I've never stayed at a hostel before and I'm glad you got a bed. It's lucky since it's a holiday." Charlotte slipped from the car, waited for him to get out before she locked the doors.

"I would have happily slept in the van but glad I don't have to."

"Let's go check it out." She stretched, walking ahead, deep in her thoughts. Her muscles were already protesting the lack of motion driving required. So far, the trip was going well but she did want some time to herself. Maybe after today they could go their separate ways during stops. He was a big boy who could entertain himself and well, she preferred to be alone. Plus, her audience awaited. Her first live broadcast on Facebook was due. She would have to send him off somewhere to do other things while she did that. His footsteps kept rhythm with hers, the crunch on the ground in sync with her own, stopping when she stopped to open the door of the Hostel to check in.

Chapter 5

"I'm sorry sir, I booked you in error. The bunk I was going put you in has a female occupant who wants only another female to share. You understand?" The contrite, red-faced clerk stared at his computer as though he could change what he read with his eyes.

"Yes, I understand there is a bed, but I can't have it." Garry raked a hand through his hair. He thought he'd settled all of this.

"I am so sorry, let me try to find you another place to stay. It's Canada Day though and everything is pretty full but if there is anything I'll find it." He picked up the phone and placed a call.

"It's me." Charley insinuated herself into the conversation. Is it my room you can only book a

female in? I checked in a few moments ago.
Charlotte Andrews."

The clerk, put his hand over the telephone
receiver and nodded, "yes, ma'am it's you. It was
showing as available so when the gentleman called I
booked him but I realize now there is a note you
would pay for the second bed if a lone female didn't
come to share it with you. Well no women are
traveling alone and it's still un-booked so you'll be
charged."

"Put Garry in the room. I know him."
Garry's face registered his surprise.

"I'm sorry, I don't understand. Really?" The
clerk hung up the phone.

"I picked him up on the way through and
he's fine, I'll share with him."

"Ma'am are you sure, I mean if you picked
him up on the way?" A worried look crossed the
clerk's face. It had been his error and if something
went wrong.

"Yeah, I'm positive, it'll be fine. We'll
share. Put it on one bill and he'll pay me after."

"Wow, that's quite a vote of confidence and
trust there. Thank you." Garry had been told to keep
his distance from her by his grandmother. Separate
rooms she had said and she had been firm. Maybe
he should sleep in the van.

"It's not trust of you, it's trusting my
grandmother and your grandmother will kill you if

you step out of line. We're adults here." She breathed deeply. She had not had a man in her room while she slept in well over a decade. Never thought she would again, now she was going to spend a night alone with one. A smiled flickered on her lips as she recalled the look of shock on the clerk's face. Pick up a stranger, share a room with him. That was not a Charlotte thing to do.

"Must be a Charley thing."

"What must be?" Garry asked, confused.

"Nothing. Just thinking out loud. I do that a lot, ignore me," she advised, unlocking the door to their room.

A simple space, it had a bunk bed, a shared bathroom, two stools and a privacy curtain.

She threw her bag on the top bunk and climbed up. She pulled out some appropriate hiking clothes, her boots still in the van.

"I need to change. Can you leave until I do?"

"Yeah, no problem." He tossed his bag on the lower bed and departed.

Charley laid back on the bunk for a moment. She hoped he didn't snore. *This was safe. This was safe.* She would be okay. She breathed in and out. She had no intuition of anything unsafe with Garry. Had she had that with Rick? She couldn't even remember her young pre-Rick self. But yeah, her intuition had been spot on, her common sense was what had deserted her back then.

She finished a short meditation, dressed and walked out to the van. Garry stared at the mountains, a trail map in his hands, boots changed.

"Ready?"

"Slight change of plans. We're going to the hot springs. Do you have a swimsuit?"

"Sure, in the back of the van. Which one?"

"Miette, let's go, do a short hike, then relax in the waters. If you don't want to go that's fine."

"I think the question is, do you want me to go with you?" Sometimes he felt she wanted to tell him to frig off and other times she seemed to be happy enough that he was here.

"Sure." Did she want him to? Not sure. Was she okay if he did. Yeah.

It took an hour to drive there and it was supper time when they reached the destination on their hike. The Fiddle Valley was fragrant and verdant green, the Rockies towering around it, reaching into the clouds that drifted at their peaks. They rested at some old hotel ruins.

"It never fails to catch me off guard, how beautiful the mountains are. But you also must admit, it stinks." Garry raised his nose in the air.

They were seated in an area called Utopia Pass, somewhat less impressive compared to the splendour of the rest of the trail but still exceptionally beautiful.

"Oh, my God, I know, rotten eggs. That's the sulfur from the springs I suppose. It's awful until you go nose-blind to it. What do we have to eat?" Charley asked. Garry had picked up food for them.

"Egg salad sandwiches," he laughed, "was that deliberate? Are we on a theme here?"

"Let's hope they're not rotten eggs." She smiled as she pulled plastic wrap aside. The sandwich was delicious, there was something different about them. Green onions, pepper, mustard, mayo. Dijon mayonnaise. She spoke it all out loud, dissecting the recipe.

"These are amazing. Just enough too. I'll still want a hot meal tonight though. So you know, I'm revising my plans a bit. I'm not going to go to Banff tomorrow. Figure I'll just drive down through and head to Calgary."

"Oh yeah? Why the change?"

"Well, I've never been to Calgary. I've hiked Banff before. I hike everywhere. I know we're supposed to have these big natural experiences as Canadians but most of us live in cities. I think I want to see what the city is all about. Spend a couple nights there."

"Alberta's interesting, different from the other provinces. Well, Alberta *and* Saskatchewan," he looked off into the distance, admiring the blue sky beyond the craggy peaks.

"Very different. There's a lot of passion about oil. But also about farming, beef is big here, and so is other agriculture. It's an odd mix. I sure hope they never find oil here." She gestured out at the mountains. Nothing was off limits if the right people were elected. Pipelines would tear through prime lands and national parks if it were up to certain business and government leaders. Yet, she had her own guilt on this. She had forgone the hybrid vehicle she first looked at for this trip and bought the Ford. She used oil and gas regularly so she could hardly judge without being hypocritical. Using fossil fuels, she conceded, to get from place to place or heating her home to stay warm was hardly the same as trying to make far more money than any human required, to the detriment of the planet. But still, she was not without guilt for it.

"Can you imagine if they did to this place what they did to Northern Alberta, the tar sands," she wondered aloud.

"I've done a lot of thinking on that and it would be terrible. But still, while it would be fantastic if we could switch over to renewable energy one hundred percent, it's not something we can do overnight and fact is, an oil center like Alberta—" Garry thoughts were aligned with hers.

"Or newfoundland," she added between bites.

"Yes, Newfoundland too, would be damaged economically by the transition. I don't want that. So, I'm torn."

"Me too. I get why people are against it. I just know it can't go on forever." She finished her sandwich.

"Should we go soak in some hot mineral water and contemplate how to fix the Alberta economy?" Garry asked.

"Or the Canadian economy?"

"Why, I hear these minerals are so therapeutic and magic, we could solve the world economy's issues," he exaggerated as he stood. He tucked his garbage into his backpack and slung it over his shoulder.

She stood and smiled up at him. They were facing each other and she felt an overwhelming urge to kiss him. She could see in the narrowing of his eyes he knew it. On an impulse, she leaned forward half a centimeter. He did the same.

"Baaaaaaa!" Charley's heart leapt in her chest and she grabbed Garry's arm. Out of reflex he pushed her behind him, standing still, facing the wild animal.

A Bighorn sheep stared at them. Its eyes blinked, the white, solid, unmoving body transfixed by the frightened humans. These large rams, with their impressive curled horns spiraling into a sharp point, were quite capable of impaling a couple of intrusive humans. Generally, though, they weren't motivated to do so.

Situated against a magnificent mountain backdrop, it would have been a breathtaking photo, had either of them attempted to snap one. Instead, the startled humans remained still, not daring to reach for their iPhones to capture the scene.

Garry spoke, just a few words his voice quiet but it was Charley's loud laugh a moment later that sent the terrified creature bounding off, white rump disappearing into the folds of the woods as though the devil himself were chasing it.

Threat gone, they collapsed, laughing against each other. Charley couldn't wait to tell this story to her followers, revising it to leave out the nearly kissing part of course. On the drive back she giggled every time she remembered what had caused her to laugh so hard she scared away the Bighorn.

"You have very baaaaad timing," Garry had said to the sheep.

Chapter 6

"This is too hot." Garry was immersed to his neck in the waters of Miette Hot Springs. Charley was beside him, deep into her thoughts. Being dragged from them set her on edge and it crept into her voice.

"They're *hot* springs."

"I know but this is scalding. I think I'm allergic," Garry lifted himself out of the water, his body red from his neck down, he scratched his chest leaving long white streaks. "I have to get out, it's too hot, it's burning my skin."

"Oh, my God, wow, yeah. There's a bottle of Benadryl in the van, go take a couple. I'll catch up with you later." Charley closed her eyes. She felt him hesitate, then grab the keys from behind her.

She listened to his retreating footsteps until he was gone. It might be a bit callous not to go along and make sure he was okay but she had promised herself he wouldn't interfere with her plans. And her plan right now was to soak. Plus, he was a big boy and could take care of himself.

The sun made had not made its final dip into the mountains yet. It warmed her upturned face. Charley's body felt like molten wax under the hot water. People climbed in and out of the pool, chatting and laughing, sending waves around her. She sunk deeper into her reverie, submerged to the tips of her ears.

Perhaps this time alone would give her the skills to cope with Garry. God, had she almost kissed him? Had she been alone so long, with no male company, she was falling all over the first man she spent time with? This wasn't like her at all. Close confines and the intimacy of conversation made him attractive to her. That was all. Plus, he was a nice-looking man, fit and healthy but it would be a bit too Harlequin Romance to fall into anything more than companionship with him.

"I could kill you Nan, honest to God."

"Pardon me?" A woman shot her a horrified look.

"Oh, no, not you." Charley's eyes popped open, she splashed upright. "I was just thinking out loud. I'm sorry. My Grandmother saddled me with this guy on my drive across the country and he's driving me a bit crazy." Charley shook her head, the tips of her hair still dipped into the water despite it being lifted-up in her baseball hat.

"What's wrong with him?" the woman, around Charley's age, pretty with short blond hair in a pixie cut she envied, asked her.

"Just him being here. He's nice enough I suppose, but I like being alone."

"You do? Hi, I'm Patsy Smythe, from Saskatoon." She said "toon" with precision.

"Yeah, I have been alone a long time and I love it."

"Not me, I hate it. Wish my grandmother would set *me* up with a guy. Is he good looking?"

"Yeah, he is. Very." She took a deep breath, "I'm Charlotte Andrews." There, she had introduced herself to a stranger.

"Maybe I should drive him across Canada. I'm desperate enough for company. It feels like I do everything alone. I had a ton of girlfriends but the last one just got married out east and I couldn't afford to make the trip. I was so depressed I decided to come up here and relax. Even though her new husband is an asshole, I'm still jealous. It's hard to meet people. And you meet them and they're jerks."

"So, you want to meet men and find it hard, and I prefer being alone and my Grandmother forces a man on me. Sounds like life." Charley rolled her eyes.

"Where is the guy now?" Patsy looked around.

"I don't know, he said the water was too hot and left. I'm not too concerned, he's a big boy, I needed to be alone for a while and recharge."

"Oh, I'm sorry, I'm interrupting you."

"No, no you're not. It's fine. I don't mind chatting, it's fine." She repeated it to convince herself it was indeed, fine. She was supposed to talk to Canadians. That was part of the trip.

"So where are you going?" Patsy settled back in the water. Both women stared ahead.

"Newfoundland, to my grandmother's place. Well the whole trip is about Canada, exploring it, discovering it and so on. But I'll end up at Nan's."

"Wow, sounds incredible. I would love to do something like that."

"I've got this blog I write about all things Canadian, I have a one-hundred percent Canadian play list, I'm looking to talk to Canadians, guess you're my first one, get to know what they're like. I was going to explore Banff as well as Jasper but I've decided to drive on through to Calgary, get to see the city a bit."

"Will you write a book about it? That's what you should do?" Patsy was excited at the prospect.

"Well Garry—that's the guy—he's taking notes, I keep a journal and do the blog so who knows? If I discover anything worthwhile, maybe.

Have any purely Canadian perspectives?" She explained the *Charley through Canada* thing, afraid it would make the woman less inclined to talk but it didn't, she seemed more excited than ever.

"I don't know. Is there such a thing? I mean I live in Saskatoon, I've never left it. I don't know if I have anything whatsoever in common with a Newfoundlander or someone from Quebec so how can you have a Canadian perspective? There are how many people in the country?"

"Thirty-five million give or take," Charley informed her.

"Right so, that's thirty-five million perspectives, right?" Patsy thought hard.

"Good point. Yeah."

"And the east has no idea about the west. We're sort of left out here alone to fend for ourselves. The only parts of Canada that matter are Ontario and Quebec as far as I can see. Whenever you see this Canadian identity thing tossed about it's always from an Ontario perspective with French subtitles."

"I think I've heard a similar sentiment in Newfoundland. Perhaps the people in the far north feel that way too."

"Yeah? Well don't get me started on the natives. They just suck billions of dollars out of the country and just waste it all, while they're off drinking."

Charley sat up, water sloshed down her arms and a warm breeze brushed across her skin as she processed the sheer racism in the woman's words. She calmed herself to listen. She was on a "fact-seeking" mission, not a "change the country" mission. Still, blood surged behind her ears as the diatribe continued.

"And the government sends a fortune to other countries. Bringing in thousands of refugees, God knows who they are and what they'll do, with our money, while we have problems at home. Saskatoon has homeless problems, why not fix that first, take care of our own?"

Charley took a deep breath. She knew the answer to the next question before she asked it.

"Do you volunteer with the homeless then?"

"Well no, I don't have much time to do that. I'm far too busy." Patsy relaxed back against the pool's edge, soaking in the waters and the sun, her spare time slated for different priorities.

"So, do you volunteer anywhere? Do you have any causes you support?" Charley wanted her to be decent in some small way. She seemed so nice at first.

"I always give a dollar at the grocery store for the children's hospital when I get groceries. I can't afford more."

"What is your work?" Charley had to change the subject. Her blood was boiling hotter than the Miette waters.

"I get Employment Insurance. I quit my last job because the supervisor was a bitch. But I'll get another one. A nice one. If there is one that hasn't been taken by an immigrant. And that's another thing. If we weren't paying our tax dollars out to the foreigners and the Indians in welfare I could get EI for longer and take my time getting a job."

"So, are they taking all the jobs or on welfare?" Charley thought it was a logical question.

"They're leeches, that's all I can say, sucking the money out of the hard-working Canadians like me and you." Patsy's voice was annoyed now. And it was at Charley this time.

"Well, I think I've soaked up enough." Charley wasn't referring to the waters. She knew her flash point had been struck. She couldn't sort the thoughts in her head down to one thing. The words lazy, entitled, bigoted and stupid were in some of them.

"Hey, you should look me up when you drive through Saskatoon, stop by, visit. I'd love to do one of your live things with you. Plus, if you don't want the man you're driving with you can leave him with me, if he's hot enough for me, that is. Pastysmyth6979@gmail.com or look me up on Facebook." She seemed to have lost all annoyance at remembering Charley was some sort of well-known blogger.

"Oh, he's hot enough for you." *He's way out of your league*, Charley thought. What the actual fuck?

With a quick wave good-bye she lifted herself out of the pool. Charley made her way to change, seething, knowing she should have said more, pointed out all the errors in this girl Patsy's words but it wouldn't have made a difference. Plus, she knew if she started in on her she would not be able to stop.

"Hey, did you enjoy your soak? All relaxed?" Garry must have been watching for her.

"Relaxed? Oh, my God, you're not going to fucking believe this." She glanced at the darkening sky. "Let's get back, I need a drink somewhere. I'll tell you all about it on the drive."

Chapter 7

A rumble of voices met them inside the door of The Jasper Brewing Company, every inch filled. Charley's stomach growled with disappointment.

"I don't think we'll get a table."

"We'll get one, hang on." Garry walked over to the bartender and had a brief conversation, leaning between two men who allowed him to insert his body between theirs, his apology for the intrusion garnering friendly nods and a raise of their glasses.

Charley couldn't hear a word but after the conversation he returned and putting his hand on the small of her back, whispered in her ear, "come with me, there is a table opening up down at the end, two fellows on their way back to the oil fields, on their last beer, they've paid their tab."

She walked through with him, skimming along the wooden tables, filled with happy people drinking an assortment of beer.

And sure enough, as they approached two men got up and noticing them waiting there, motioned for Charley and Garry to take their seats. Friendly nods and smiles were exchanged as they sat.

"So, we can get food here for sure? I'm starved and I think the beer will knock me for a loop if I drink it on an empty stomach."

"Could last year," Garry replied," limited menu but wings, poutine, nachos."

"Good," and the waitress was there then, to take their order, her patience evident as she waited for them.

"I'll have a sleeve of the *SixtySixty Stout*, poutine, wings too, also nachos. We could just share all of that if you think you want more but I am starved and I can't decide." She closed the menu.

"Add on another poutine, we'll share the wings and nachos."

Their drinks arrived and at the taste of the stout Charley's eyes closed in pleasure.

"You like beer?"

"Never met a beer I didn't like." She took another taste.

"Me either." His laughter was a low rolling sound.

"You still itchy? I have the Benadryl in my purse."

"Yeah, a little but I'm good for now. Can't believe I'm allergic to water."

"Maybe because it's so hot and has so much sulfur? I don't know but it's better than being allergic to beer. This stuff is amazing, I'm going to try a different kind, what do you think sounds good?" She handed him the beer list.

"On your honeymoon folks?" The waitress set their food down on the table.

"Oh no, we're just traveling together. "Did she look all swoony or something? Did Garry?

"Oh, I'm sorry."

"It's fine, *fine*," Charley reassured.

Garry laughed, then winked and said, "we're an old married couple, don't believe her. She's always denying being married to me."

"But we're not—"

"Don't bother babe, she's on to you." Garry took a swig of his beer.

"Oh, that's too funny you guys and good for you, have fun, enjoy and let me know anything you need." She tripped off to the next table.

"You arse!" Charley smacked him but she grinned.

"Domestic Abuse!" he joked. His smile drifted away at her silence.

"Hey, did I say something wrong?"

"No, no, it's fine." She shook her head. This was not something she wanted to talk or even think about right now.

"Look, I'm sorry. I hit a nerve. You changed just then. I was only kidding."

"I know, don't worry about it. I know you were. I just don't find it to be that funny of a joke."

"It probably wasn't, let's talk about something else." He asked about her plans for the next few days.

The waitress returned to check on them and they ordered more drinks. Garry got serious again after she left.

"How is this going for you? Am I totally ruining this trip? I know this isn't what you had planned and I'm not the best company."

Charley took a moment, chewing on a mouthful of poutine. She knew they said the best poutine was in Quebec and if so she couldn't wait to find out because if it was better than this, wow.

"This is fucking delicious," she said, "and yes, you're ruining the entire trip."

"Oh." Garry's crestfallen face was partially hidden behind his glass of beer. "I can get another ride but I don't want to."

"Oh, my, the look on your face. It's been one friggin' day. You haven't ruined my trip. I have to say, this isn't how I planned it, you ruined my *idea* of the trip but I'm readjusting and getting used to you."

"And I don't stink."

"There's that. Do you snore?"

"Like a chainsaw."

"Me too. Well more like a jigsaw…whirr-whirr-whirr."

"I think a chainsaw is louder. I win."

"We'll have separate rooms after tonight, this beer is God-damn good."

"You curse a lot."

"I sure fucking do. When I'm not on Bowen Island."

"What? Does it have a no cursing bylaw or something?"

"Nope, I'm just respectable there, it's a small town. I try to blend in, not get noticed, fade into the background."

"So, you are yourself, like this, among your close friends?" He caught her eyes, held them. How could this woman possibly fade into the background?

"I don't have close friends." She broke away from his stare.

"You're one of those women with one very best friend who knows all her secrets are you? Like Oprah and Gail?"

"You watch Oprah?"

"Hell yeah, well when she had her show, I watch OWN now sometimes." He drained his beer. He'd had a lot of time for a while and enjoyed watching. It even helped.

"You're the first man I've ever known who admitted to that?"

"And you just changed the subject. Oprah warned about deflection like that. So, one very best bosom friend? What's she like?"

"I don't have any friends, not one. I have school colleagues, fellow teachers who I do the odd social thing with but I don't have a confidante kind of friend."

"That's not," he struggled for a word to replace 'normal', "*usual*, is it?"

"It's how I prefer it. I'm independent."

"So, you're a loner, all alone, don't you get lonely?" He shifted in his chair thinking how often he got lonely.

"I think you've used all the derivatives of alone there are. Want the Latin? '*All Ane*, from old English *all ana*. All by oneself. Wholly oneself.' I am completely whole by myself. And I like being alone. It's better."

"Wow. Latin? Aren't you the smarty-pants." He winked, impressed.

"I read stuff." She took a swig of beer and rolling her eyes in appreciation.

"And better?" He pondered for a moment. "So let's say you have a terrible problem. Who do you call for help? For support?" Garry wiped his hands in the napkin. He was truly interested in this.

"I don't call anyone. I handle it." She accepted her third beer, a *Jasper the Bear Ale*, named after the town mascot. She was somewhat glowing from the first two but she wanted to try them all.

"You handle it? Always, all alone. In Latin even. You don't talk your problems out, ask for advice."

"No, I'm capable."

"It has nothing to do with capable, we all need support. Everybody does."

"I don't."

"That's ridiculous, say you were depressed, feeling suicidal?"

"Guess I'd either do myself in or call nine-one-one.

"Don't even joke about that."

"Look I don't have friends, I can't help if you think that's pathetic. Now you're ruining my trip." Her voice elevated over the buzz of the room. A few people at the table nearby quietened.

Garry stood down. He realized he was pushing. He recalled the women he had known, each with a gaggle of girlfriends, including Helen with whom he had lived for a few years before she found a better option. She had a best friend and those two told each other when they had their last bowel movements for Christ sake. And this woman claimed to have zero friends. It was not normal.

"I'm sorry." He worried his bottom lip with his teeth.

"I'm just not good at making friends." Tears welled in her eyes, she drank again, trying to cover. "So, Mr. Know-it all, do you have a bosom buddy you like to tell every secret to? Or is it just women who must have a close friend? If men can do without why can't a woman?" She was combative.

"I have several friends who I tell a variety of different things to, so, yeah. Mostly they're from the force. But I didn't used to. It helps a great deal to have confidantes though."

Damn, he had made her cry. He felt like such an asshole. He wondered if he should mention his primary confidante, the one who knew all his secrets, the one he depended on when his life spiraled out of control and who had brought him back from the brink of disaster so that today he was a functioning, albeit damaged man. No. They had a lot of country to drive across yet and he wasn't sure she was ready to hear his life story. Perhaps she would find him pathetic for needing to have the support she claimed she could live without.

"Well that's good for you but I'm fucking fine the way I am. I have a happy life, and I enjoy it. It's safe, quiet and perfect." She slammed her drink down a bit too hard. It was the life she had created and she was happy in it. She didn't need some stranger she had barely known for twelve hours to try to convince her otherwise. Plus, she was Charley, online, with thousands of followers who supported her and kept her mind off the fact she was indeed, often, lonely as hell.

"I'm sorry Charley, I didn't mean to upset you. Please forgive me."

Charley nodded. She didn't like being challenged but he had her thinking too. Was he right? Perhaps she did need friends. She had pushed every person who might have been one away. Perhaps she needed to make an effort again. Change. It would be nice to have a friend to talk to about personal stuff. Perhaps this was something else to work on, after the trip was over.

Chapter 8

Her breathing slowed with deliberate effort. Charley inhaled and exhaled to control the panic. She'd protected her privacy with such fierceness for so many years that, while she was excited to be free of the worries that chained her to her quiet life, it was a frightening proposition to out herself to a great number of people. The event was well planned. The marketing built it up with great fanfare but now she was scared to death. Not about the content, but about everyone knowing the face behind the words. She opened her eyes after a few moments, only slightly calmer. What if it all failed? What if all the followers she had amassed over the years hated her and turned on her? Well, she'd deal with that. The time for her public debut was now. Plus, it would only be a few hundred, maybe a thousand people who would tune in.

There was a tiny part of her mind that feared nobody would tune in.

Determined, Charley fixed her hair, checked her teeth, cleared her throat and hit the Facebook Live button on her iPad.

With over one-hundred-thousand followers on her page and after sending a notification to her email list there were people waiting when she went live a few seconds later. They had never seen Charley before, not even a photo. They'd only read her witty, sometimes serious, often provocative comments on her blog. A wave of hearts flew across the screen. Her voice excited, she started in on her short speech.

"Hi everybody, and welcome. This is me, the real live, actual Charley, finally reporting in from my grand trip across the country in celebration of Canada's one hundred and fifty years of confederation. It has already been quite the adventure and I'm only here in Jasper. It is an absolute pleasure to meet you all this way. This is a whole new experience for me, because, as you know, I usually just write on the blog and nobody can see me. Often, I'm in my jammies, my hair rammed up in a clip, my googly reading glasses on with no makeup and a glass of wine next to me as I hammer out some words I think you'll all like. Now though, I had to get camera-ready. Even put on a bit of lipstick.

For those who are new, I'm Charley and I write a blog, called *Through Canada*, where I celebrate all things Canadian. I share links, we talk politics and entertainment and have a lot of fun. There is a link to the blog in the description below. Right now, I'm on a cross-country trip in celebration of Canada's 150th birthday. And I decided to do video along the way using Facebook Live. Please Like and Share my page to follow the *Charley through Canada* trip. You could win one of these T-shirts." Charley stood so the viewing audience could see hers.

"So here we go, from Jasper at a hostel I'm staying at, the first update. Oh, and I have these," she held up and glanced at the first of the stacked index cards.

"I know I told you all I would be traveling alone. Well that changed. I picked up a hitch-hiker. Isn't that crazy? I know what you're all thinking, it's horrible to pick up strangers. But not to worry, I know this is a safe country but I've not gone completely crackers. A fellow needed a ride and let's just say a friend of mine, and her friend, have vouched for his character. He's also a former RCMP officer so he'll be my guard against dangerous predators like beavers, bears and moose. That could be quite useful."

She slipped into a serious voice, eyes dead in the camera with a suspenseful pause before she spoke again. It was enough time to note the large number of viewers by the little eye icon on the screen before she spoke again.

"In fact, he already has. Earlier today he saved me from a bighorn sheep who tried to pull the wool over my eyes. That's right. I was in gravy danger but he handled it like it was mutton. He really showed his police chops. He just lambasted it with the ramifications of its baaaaaad behavior. Once he had gotten it to flock off, he gave me some great advice. He told me you can't be a sheep at the wheel when these things happen."

She gave the screen a sidelong look as if imparting the most important information of all.

"Then he said to me, 'bet ewe didn't think this cud happen. I think we best hoof it out of here.'"

A snicker escaped her and she shook off the urge to break into giggles. Her puns had been part of her blog for a long time and were met with groans and laughs equally. The views were increasing and people were sharing and sending the laugh smileys all over the screen. She decided to change her pace a bit and, with a laugh, moved on to the next topic.

"Now on a more serious note, it has been good to have company today. This guy wants to remain anonymous but we are having great conversations. Hopefully he won't be the only person I get to talk with as we travel. And he did find a nice appropriate quote for me by J. Monroe Thorington that goes, *'We were not pioneers ourselves, but we journeyed over old trails that were new to us, and with hearts open. Who shall distinguish?'* Thorington was a visitor from the United States who traveled through the Canadian Rockies and his feelings express my own as I hiked through those trails and sat in a hot spring pool in Miette. There is such a sense of the magnitude of the earth in the mountains. There is a feeling of being the first and only to experience it."

She glanced at the screen, people seemed to be engaged and the numbers were going up.

"Now let's hop to another topic. One thing I looked forward to was the driving. Most of this trip will be spent seeing things from the seat of the car, rather than on foot. And so, I prepared a very Canadian playlist.

You know from past posts that I love music. As Gordon Downie said, *'Music is the ultimate medium for expressions of love, and those expressions find a beautiful backdrop in the environment. Music is also a popular rallying point — at its central core, it's a way for people to get in touch with the best parts of themselves and to voice the love in their hearts. And the environment is one of the great loves of our lives — when we think of the best parts of ourselves, the environment is always there, informing us, as a backdrop.'* So, I'm enjoying Alanis and Celine and The Hip, Great Big Sea, Spirit of the West, Bare Naked Ladies and so on. Now my companion, he's into Justin Bieber, who I like but not like this guy. It's all Bieber all the time. You just don't expect that from a tall, strapping Mountie right? But anyway, this Mountie's a Belieber and that's okay." She smiled as she thought of Garry's reaction to that line and hoped he was watching.

"As you know, I love to hike, I love nature and I love music so that quote speaks to me in every way but it crossed my mind when I pulled into the parking lot at our place here in Jasper that there is more to Canada than I will ever see or experience. My trip excludes the north and I feel someday I'll have to visit our territories as a second part to this trip. I'll just be touching base in most places that I am going to so what I'm looking for, I may never find. I may never get a sense of this country in any real way, but that can't stop me from trying."

It was time to wind down her broadcast.

"One final thing I want to share. My friend and I discussed Canadian film. We discovered there is a long list of films we hadn't heard of. I have a question, some homework for you. What do you like or dislike about Canadian films? What is your favourite Canadian film? Leave a comment below and also share this video and your name will be entered for a chance to win a *Charley through Canada* T-shirt like the one I'm wearing." She stood once more to show her white T-shirt with the little maple leaf and logo of her blog. Then sitting down, she concluded.

"This is *Charley through Canada*, reporting from Alberta, but before I go I have a confession to make. I'm feeling awful about those puns at the start of the broadcast. I have to admit, it's kinda left me feeling a little bit sheepish."

She grinned before tapping the button to end the recording. She resisted the urge to check the comments, she would do that later and announce the

T-shirt winners at the next broadcast. She let out a breath wondering if the whole live broadcast thing had been a mistake but it was done now, everybody could put her face to the name Charley. She wasn't anonymous anymore. She felt a thrill and good idea or not, she was enjoying herself.

In spite of her companion, this was going very well.

Chapter 9

The paralysis struck about twenty minutes after she climbed into the top bunk. It rammed into her mind first, throwing every possible potential bad thing that could happen, before her. They were memories and possibilities all rolled into one great jumble that terrified her in the dark room. Before she could talk her mind out of thinking the thoughts, the emotions associated with them battered her. Charley gasped for breath, pupils dilated, limbs chained to the bunk.

She'd felt she could handle sharing a room with Garry, hadn't even thought about it being a problem in any real sense, but the moment her head descended onto the thick pillow she'd been gripped by a sense of impending doom unlike any she had felt since her marriage ended.

For what seemed like hours she was tossed like a rag doll back into other dark rooms, on other nights, so long ago when she had been in real and imminent danger. Back to a time when the man in her life posed a genuine threat to her physical safety and no matter how she talked to herself, there was an intense feeling of despair sharing the bunk with her. It breathed when she breathed, turned over when she turned and watched without mercy as she wept into her pillow.

High above the floor, on her back, facing the ceiling she prayed. It didn't help. The moments dragged like a cantankerous child, hanging limp, not budging. She turned to her side to relieve a knot that had formed in her lower back from being in the same position for so long. She prayed some more.

Charley checked the time on her phone. Had it only been only twelve minutes since she last looked? It was nearly 4:30am and she only drifted once, her body lulled into slumber by the slowness of time and the weight of her fear. But, in just moments the creak of someone walking outside awakened her, heart pounding, palms sweating. She cursed at herself. Tried thinking herself down again.

Garry is asleep. The danger is nearly two decades ago. There is nothing to be afraid of.

Her body disagreed. She turned the opposite way, facing the wall, ears on high alert, stress level rising. She couldn't turn her back. So she flipped over once more, this time with a sigh. Insomnia was one thing, this heavy, unwarranted dread was another entirely.

Did this mean she would never be able to sleep with a man in her room again? Maybe she hadn't waited long enough, gotten to know Garry more before sharing the room. But her instincts had declared him safe, it was her past trauma that was causing her to feel terror where there was nothing to fear.

Her foot poked out from underneath the blanket and touched something at the foot of the bed, and she recoiled. She scolded herself. It was just her purse.

Her purse! She had Benadryl in there. Maybe that would help her sleep. She sat up and reached, her body leaning close to the wall. She couldn't even hear Garry breathing, much less snoring. God, if only it was just snoring that kept her awake.

She located the white bottle and shook a pill into her hand. Then added another. Insurance. She popped the pink tablets into her mouth and swallowed. They were smooth and small and slipped down without effort. She recapped the bottle and made her way back to her pillow, the pill bottle still grasped tight, held like a weapon. She understood how people became addicted. She only had access to Benadryl but she would have taken anything available to ease this feeling.

Charley curled into a fetal position and waited, hoping it would at least relax her until the feeling of dread subsided.

A while later she awakened, body leaden, a fog over her brain. She slipped in and out of sleep for a while longer, the fear gone but the effects of the pills not allowing her to fully rouse.

Finally, the urge to use the bathroom overcame her need for sleep and at around seven she descended the ladder then climbed back up a short while later, still exhausted.

Garry still slept, harmless as a kitten. There had never been anything real to fear. Nobody had told her mind and body however.

On the next awakening he was gone. Likely well-rested and ready. Charley slept again after a moment of resentment. It would be another hour before she could function.

Extra coffee. That would be necessary if they were to safely make it to Calgary. Showered, dressed, she was ready for the road when he showed up.

"Hey, you're ready? I was going to sneak in and get my bag. I brought you a Timmie's." He handed her the large cup.

"Oh, my God thank you." A shaking hand grabbed the cup, resentment sold for a dark roast.

"You're welcome. I've eaten, but I'll go with you, keep you company." His smile held pleading. He still felt bad about upsetting her the night before. He also worried about her. One day with Charley and he felt protective of her which was silly. He couldn't protect anybody anymore. But at least he could try not to cause harm.

"I'm okay with coffee until we stop again." Her stomach knotted, her appetite non-existent, perhaps from the night of terror she had just endured, or maybe from the pills she had ingested. Either way, she wasn't ready for food.

A short time later they checked out and loaded the van, day two of their trip before them. Charley yawned as she climbed into the driver's seat.

"I can drive if you like," Garry offered, his smile warm, his eyes concerned.

"I'm fine, it's not far."

"If you're sure, I'm here if you need me," and he didn't mean to drive.

Charley understood. "Thank you. That's nice."

It was. And while Charley yearned to be extraordinary, to do bigger, more important things, after the torture of the previous night, this kind of ordinary morning was a pretty attractive place.

Chapter 10

"You know I can drive, right? I have a valid driver's license and I can do turns like *The Dukes of Hazard*. Want me to take over?" Garry offered again after another great yawn when they stopped to fuel up and for her to eat.

"That's not reassuring."

"It is if we get chased by the police." He pronounced it po-lease with a southern drawl.

"I know what this is about. It's not because I'm tired, it's because you noticed I always set my cruise to exactly the speed limit and it's driving you crazy, right? Some cop you are!"

"Well, yeah, you *could* go faster," he nodded. It was the first time he had ever told somebody to speed.

"Well Mr. Mountie, if you drive my car you have to go the speed limit and I don't think you can do that. I'm a law-abiding citizen you know."

"You might be the first person under forty I've ever known who drives the speed limit and I know precious few over forty."

"I'm forty-four."

"Seriously?"

"No, I'm thirty-seven."

"Still too high." He stared at her. She couldn't be more than early thirties tops.

"I'm forty-four. True story."

"Okay, you drive."

"Because I'm forty-four?" She shot him a quizzical look as she hopped back in and buckled up. She'd managed to eat some breakfast and grab another coffee.

"No because I have to make a call." He tapped his phone as she pulled out of the parking lot.

"Oh, okay."

"Morning Nan." He glanced at Charley and grinned.

She listened to the one-sided conversation, amused.

"Oh yes, I forgot the time difference. What's for dinner? God love ya, she's making toutons." The latter was intended for Charley.

"We're heading to Calgary I think." His eyes queried Charley who nodded.

"No, she changed her mind about Banff. Yes we're fine. Yes I'm good and behaving. I feel fine, no it's nice, relaxing. Yes, I like her. Nan she's right here. No I s'pose it's no big deal if she knows I like her but what if I didn't? Then I'd have to say I like her anyway so Nan you really don't know if I like her or not for sure."

Charley giggled. Poor Ger.

"Nan, I have a question for you." He waited for a reply. It took far longer than a yes should have. Charley was curious but kept her eyes on the road.

"What is Charley's middle name?"

"What?" Charley snapped.

"Okay, also how old is she?" He nodded at the answer, his eyes widening.

"Really, she looks much younger. Yeah, three years or so."

"Oh, my God, you're nervy." She kept her voice low. She wanted to swear at him but his nan was on the phone.

"OK Nan, we're fine. I'll call you in a few days okay?" He didn't hang up.

"Okay, I'll call you tomorrow if we have signal." Still he held the phone.

"Okay Nan, I'll call you from the hotel phone if we don't have signal. Okay, yes, we had a big supper last night and breakfast this morning. The food has been good. Nan—look, no Nan I don't need money. It's all straightened away now. I got it all. I told you . Bye, I love you. Bye." He listened for a while longer then, said bye again and clicked the button.

"You asked your Nan how old I am?"

"Nan says hello."

"You didn't believe me? What gall!"

"You don't look your age."

"I do, this is what forty-four looks like."

"You're older than me."

"I'm older than many people. All of them under forty-four. So, that's likely."

"I just turned forty-one."

"Oh, well you'll be just right next year."

"What? Just right for what?"

"You'll be the best male age, the most attractive."

Charley was enjoying his confusion a bit too much but it served him right, he started this.

"Forty-two. It's when men are the most attractive, grown up, ready to settle. Desirable."

"You have a preferred age for men? Is that usual, do all women?"

"I don't know. I told you I don't have any friends. But personally, it's about right. They are seasoned, a touch of grey, you know if they're going to lose their hair or not, not that it matters but at least you know. Plus, they've already fucked up a few relationships and are showing signs of growth or lack of growth so, yeah, that's the age. You're not there yet tom cod." She turned, gave him a wink and a nod before looking back at the road.

"That is the strangest thing I've ever heard."

"I once knew a guy who stunk so bad, it was like he wiped his ass back to front so he stank all the time. We called him Smelly Scrotum. That's far stranger than men being perfectly mature at forty-two."

Garry was silent and Charley glanced his way to see he was choking on something. He wheezed, then snorted, a sound that morphed into a great guffaw, shoulders heaving and eyes dripping. He pulled off his sunglasses, wiping his face with the back of his hand, tried to speak but his ability to do so had vanished.

"What?" Charley asked, her tone dead serious.

"That—" and Garry was gone again, unable to stop.

Charley snickered and tried to keep her giggles to herself.

"What?" she asked more firmly, "you said it was the strangest thing you ever heard. I knew there were stranger things. Like, once there was a guy walking down my street carrying a bar of soap, his hand flat, the soap on top of it, singing at the top of his lungs, *'Once more, you open the door and you're here in my heart and my heart goes on and on,'* you know, that song from *The Titanic* that Celine Dion—a Canadian I might add—sang? That's a strange thing too. Surely there are many things stranger than a man being at his peak attractiveness at forty-two."

"Okay," snort, "you're right. I have now heard *two* stranger things. Let me catch my—" and he was gone again, the amusement overtaking him as she drove along, a touch of mirth on her lips but otherwise not seeming to find her own comments as hilarious as he did.

"You're funny," he finally managed after catching his breath again.

"I'm a god-damned riot," she agreed.

"Why forty-two? Why not forty? Or forty-four?" He caught his breath and could get the words out.

"I don't know, ask the creator of ages. It is forty-two that is the prime. What is it for women?"

"I think it has to be forty-four. Because you're a fucking miracle." He snorted again, then recovered.

"And you know it," she stated, pulling over into the lane and setting the cruise for five kilometers over the speed limit.

Garry was still wiping his eyes from laughing when he noticed.

"Slow down, speed demon," he commanded, before falling into hysterical laughter once more.

This time Charley joined him.

Chapter 11

"You don't have to pay, this is far more expensive than last night." Charley looked about the Calgary Tower. She was excited about the dinner but didn't want to be beholden.

"I know I don't have to pay. It's no wonder you don't have any friends. You're difficult. I want to eat here since we're not going to the Stampede. Can't we do anything I want?" He pouted, then winked and went off to look at some postcards calling her over after a few moments. "I'm not hanging out here for two weeks to see a bunch of cowboys and horses," he mimicked what she'd said when he mentioned it, then showed her the postcard of just that. "I'm going to mail one of these cards to Nan, from Canada's highest mailbox. She'll get a kick out of it."

"Oh, I have to get one for Nan too. I should mail postcards the entire time from everywhere.

That would be fun for her." Charley looked at some mountain scenes.

"Copycat," he kidded.

She showed him her choice, a panorama of western mountains beyond the cityscape. I want a souvenir for her too. Something small. A fridge magnet. Nan would like that."

"I'd better get one too then—might not have a place to live if I don't treat my Nan as good as you treat yours, they'll be talking."

"You better Garry or it'll be *'Oh, yeah, well, Charlotte brought me this fridge magnet from Calgary,' 'oh , Garry didn't bring me anything, out he goes tomorrow!'* She did her best imitation of the two women.

"Exactly. By the way Nan told me you're Charlotte Anne Nova? That's your full name?"

"Damn your grandmother! Yeah, mom was born with a romantic streak, or a geography streak. I was named after the province in which I was born, Nova Scotia and the city where I was conceived, Charlottetown. The Anne is from Anne of Green Gables."

"Wow, so why don't you use Charlotte all the time then? Why the short form?" Garry paid for his items, purchased two stamps and started writing something on his postcard. "What's the postal code?"

"A0G 1R0." She addressed hers also. "I'm always called Charlotte when I'm home on Bowen Island."

"I'm never Garrison. That's my real first name."

"Garrison. Yes, I knew that. Garrison what? You know my middle names. I should know yours."

"Promise you won't laugh?"

"No of course I won't promise. I'm going to bug you about it forever even if it's something normal like Thomas."

"It's Ford." He waited. It only took a moment.

"Your god-damned name is Garrison Ford, rhymes with Harrison Ford? No way, that is a lie, that is a fucking lie."

"Shhh!" He pulled her over to mail the cards, then towards the observation deck, laughing.

"You're a liar right?"

"Here." He flipped his wallet open and there it was. Garrison Ford Clarke right on his driver's license.

"Let's boldly go, Garrison Ford. Was it deliberate? Did your mother know? This is epic. I can't believe it. Why am I calling you Garry when I could be calling you Han Solo? Garrison is a great name by the way, and Ford, also, a great name but together they are the very best!"

"I was born before the first movie, but my mother was already a fan so yeah, deliberate and *Boldly Go* is Star Trek, not Star Wars. And I don't tell everybody and the last girl I told didn't get it at all."

"Oh right. So she never watched Star Wars uh?"

"Want a confession? *I've* never watched Star Wars."

"No flippin' way, your name is Garrison Ford and you haven't watch Star Wars."

"I know, crazy right? But I have watched Indiana Jones films!"

"Garrison, look at that!" She used his full name, pointing over the city

"Oh, spectacular eh?"

They walked out on the observation deck as they were chatting and the entire city was spread out before them.

"This is wonderful. Maybe we'll do the CN Tower in Toronto too."

"Look at those mountains Charlotte?" He pointed towards them in the distance.

"I should have brought my camera." She ignored his calling her Charlotte. He'd get lazy and go back to Charley, she hoped.

"Let's do a selfie!" He pulled out his phone. He was like a boy sometimes.

"Together? Or I take a pic of you and you take one of me?"

"Well that's not a selfie now is it. No let's do one together."

They huddled in, the sun in the west making it a bit too dark to get it against the backdrop of the mountains so he hit a filter on the phone and tried that. It came out clear and bright, their two smiling faces with the majesty of the Rockies behind them. He texted it to her.

"I love this, I'm putting it on Facebook. On my private timeline, not on the public page," she reassured him.

"I'll add you as a friend then you can tag me in it."

"Okay." She uploaded and accepted his request noting his profile pic was a photo of him much younger, in full RCMP regalia, the scarlet jacket, black pants with its recognizable yellow stripe, black boots and hat.

"Perfect." He accepted her request.

"Nice picture, very handsome," Charley said.

"Woohoo! I've been upgraded from cute to handsome." He twirled, shaking his butt and doing some sort of weird happy dance.

She stuck her tongue out at him.

"Soooo mature, come on," he joked, then checked his phone, "five minutes to the reservation. Let's go!"

The Sky 360 restaurant overlooked the city. They absorbed the panoramic view as the waiter took their order and brought their wine.

"It's good to go out to a nice place occasionally." Charley said.

"I likes doing it up all fancy on times b'y,"

"You're not good at the dialect. You were away too long."

"I didn't grow up in Newfoundland, I never had a dialect. We moved there when I was fourteen from Ontario. I moved away again when I was eighteen."

"Twillingate right?"

"New World Island. Not far from you."

"Now your Grandmother has a house on Change Islands near my grandmother. Funny how things go."

"Oh, this looks amazing." She moved back to allow the food to be served. Their appetizers were an Alberta Meeze for two with hummus and an Olive Tapenada, baquette, polenta fries. It was all French and Eastern Europe inspired and delicious. They started in.

"I won't have room for the entrée."
Charlotte set her napkin on her lap and leaned in,
eyeing the fare.

"Yeah you will, and dessert too, let's get fat
and enjoy our food."

"I do enjoy food, I eat what I like."

"Still, you're so small."

"I hike a lot, I don't eat a lot of junk food
except for Diet Doctor Pepper and I only eat meals.
No snacks. Except when driving. Anything goes
when I'm on a trip."

"Sounds like a good attitude. And healthy."

"It is. I hope. I never get sick." She sipped at
some ice water. Where had the fun conversation
gone?

"I have a question for you Charlotte." He
cast his eyes down, his expression guarded.

"Shoot." She popped a bit of hummus-
dipped bread into her mouth and waited.

"What is this trip about for you? Aside from
the Facebook thing and the blog I mean, seriously,
what did you set out to do? You wanted to discover
things about the country you say but I sense it's
more personal than that. I know I'm not interfering
in the work side of things but maybe on the personal
side, I'm in the way?"

"Well," she took another sip of wine and let
it slide, enjoying it," damn this is good Garrison,
and, um, well, oh yeah, your question. I don't know.

Well I guess I know but, we're still touring Canada, there is a whole lot of driving left to do, and you certainly were unexpected but then, this whole trip was about discovery and doing the unexpected. So far, you've been logical and reasonable, you're funny, you do shut up long enough in the car for me to get inside my own head and do my thinking which is part of what I want to do, contemplate." She took a deep breath. He hadn't asked for as much information as she'd given.

The waiter brought their entrees, setting braised bison back ribs in front of her and placing a delicious-looking strip sirloin of Alberta beef in front of him.

"Thank you," she addressed the waiter, then looked at Garry, took another deep breath and said what she was thinking, "I kind of like having the company."

"Do you like me?" His eyes twinkled and he grinned but the question wasn't as casual as he pretended.

"Alright, geez, yes, I suppose I like you."

"She likes me!" He raised his hand and the waiter who finished topping up their wine gave him a high five. "You know I was barely tolerable in Vancouver and now she likes me."

"But does she *'like'* like you?" the waiter asked, with a conspiratorial wink.

"Oh, it's too soon," Charley answered, not as annoyed as she should be by being put on the spot, "it'll be at least Quebec City before I can answer that."

"L'amour est dans l'air," the waiter responded

"Oh j'espere vraiment que oni," Garry replied.

"Wait, what?" said Charley.

Chapter 12

"It would have made more sense to go to Edmonton first, then down to Calgary but I want to go to Lloydminster also and then across that way to Saskatoon and this way we were able to at least drive down through to Banff," Charley explained.

"The route is up to you." He set the navigation system for Drumheller, Alberta.

"Don't you think it's strange how the world surprises you?"

"What do you mean specifically?"

"Well," Charley said, "I spent a lot of my time in a place so wrapped up in its geology, ancient Maritime Archaic artifacts are found all over the area, and the place proves the continental divide, and I thought we had dibs on an extraordinary and rich ancient heritage. But here, out in a place I had never heard of they have the remains of giant dinosaurs."

"Which were manufactured and are a big hoax."

"What?"

"Well there are people who actually don't believe in them. Creationists who think this is all fabricated. Hey not me, conservative as I am, I like my science."

"You're a conservative? As in *Stephen Harper* conservative?"

"Well, I wasn't a fan of his in particular. But I did vote for him. I preferred the old Progressive Conservative Party. Don't tell me you're a Liberal."

"Of course, I'm a Liberal. I am a big Trudeaumaniac. Also, since you voted for Stephen Harper, the man who nearly destroyed this democracy, the most hateful, vindictive, spiteful, scum ever elected in this great country, you'll have to walk the rest of the way. There is nobody more anti-Canadian than Stephen Harper and if you're a supporter of his you'll have to get out." She hit the signal light, pulled over, slipped the Ford into park and waited.

Her face was stone serious. He lost his smile and his voice was tentative as he asked, "you're that serious about politics?"

"I'm that serious about Canada. Get out."
She stared straight ahead, waiting.

"Charley," he breathed, "isn't this a bit of an over-reaction?"

Traffic whizzed by. He considered his options. This woman was nuts. He was better off taking his chances with the highway. And he'd be damned if he'd beg her. He reached for the door handle.

"Oh, my God, you idiot!" Charley's face split into a big grin. It soon turned into great wails of laughter that had her shoulders heaving.

He leaned back, shook his head. Damn her.

"I can't stop, you may have to drive," she gasped.

"I'm going to get you." He joined her, his deep laugh joyful. "Seriously, I am going to get you back, I don't know how, but I will."

She heaved the SUV in drive and pulled back out onto the highway. "I do think Stephen Harper was a close call."

"You think sunshine boy is better?"

"I think he's a nicer person who cares about people. I don't think he's perfect, but there is no perfect person for any job. He has done some things I don't care for, I'll admit. But he is promoting women's issues and that is a huge deal for me. Yes, there are some things he should have been smarter about. I want him to succeed but only so much that the country succeeds. I never vote Conservative due to their stances on social issues like immigration and gay rights but they have taken an extreme step backwards these past few years. I think if I wanted my party to win rather than the country be successful than I'd be happy with that, but I would prefer if all our politicians accepted human rights, women's rights and so on and simply battled on how to move forward on policy about the economy and democracy and fairness."

"I'm not going to argue politics because, frankly, I vote and that's it. I have no problem with gay marriage, immigration, refugees, I simply don't know much about the whole thing. But I do think we have to be careful who we let into the country."

"We already are careful. I think we need to be careful about people already living here. Like taking strangers into your car and driving across the country with them. You never know what sort of secrets they have lurking under the surface. We've been driving for a few days and all I know about you is you're a former Mountie with a funny name. But I would have given you the ride if your family came from Syria or Iraq or Korea, if my Nan and yours said you were okay. Perhaps our Nans should vet the refugees and immigrants that come over?"

"Fair point, and yeah, that would be a much safer option." He grinned at the idea.

"So, what is it? What are your secrets Han Solo? Why couldn't you fly home? Why aren't you a cop anymore?"

Something heavy shifted and Charley felt its weight. She had struck a nerve and he was angered. Or frightened. She couldn't tell.

"What, only cops get to interrogate?" she asked.

"Something like that."

"Alright, don't tell me your darkest, deepest secrets," Maybe it wasn't fair to ask but she was sure damned curious now.

His face relaxed, relieved.

"But give me something, tell me about your life, where you've lived. You're in your forties, you've been in the RCMP, you must have a story," she went on.

"Okay, well it's kind of boring." He exhaled. He could do that.

"I'll act delighted and intrigued, I swear." She raised two fingers in what was supposed to be some sort of pledge. "I think that means I promise." She shrugged.

"Well, I was born in Southwestern Ontario, Tavistock is the town. It's near Stratford, where the Beebs was born, but my parents were from Newfoundland, Dad worked at the cheese factory there and mom was home with us, volunteered at the school, and wrote for the local paper sometimes."

"Near the Beebs! We should go there! On the trip, do you want to go to Tavistock?" she inquired, having heard of the place.

"That would be great. I've never been back but I keep in touch with a friend from there on Facebook. We moved to Summerford when I was fourteen and I graduated and hightailed it out of there for Ontario again. I hated it the entire time. I appreciate it now but then, it was awful, mostly because of my age and missing my friends but I did like being near my Grandparents. As a teen, though, grandparents aren't as important as your buddies."

"That is completely understandable."

"So, then I went to University in Ottawa, graduated with a degree in business, decided I hated it before ever taking a job and joined the RCMP. I was with them until last year. Though I've been off on leave for several years."

"You retired early?"

"I was injured which led to a disability which led to an early retirement." That was all he would say. He was out of the force. He had been an officer almost twenty years. That was enough information. He should have had another ten at least.

"What sort of injury?" She scanned his physique. He looked fit and healthy now.

"Gun shot, not seriously wounded but there were complications." He shifted in his seat, tried not to remember that day, how he had almost died. The small scar from his wound had healed, it was barely visible. *It* hadn't ended his career. It was the other wounds, the ones he didn't mention that caused that.

"Wow, I'm shocked though, I suppose it happens even in Canada. I'm glad we have the gun laws we do but the wrong people always find a way. Look you don't have to talk about this if you don't want to, I didn't know it was all this serious, but let me ask you this instead. How do law enforcement people feel about gun laws generally?" She squirmed. She'd never known anybody who was shot.

"Gun laws wouldn't have helped what happened in my situation but I think the stricter the better, that's my opinion. I can't speak for other officers but fewer guns being in the hands of anybody civilian is better. It's rare but not impossible for a police officer to get shot in this country, it's common in the US. They are the most ridiculous country ever when it comes to guns. If there is one thing I feel good about driving around in Canada is hardly anybody has a gun in their glove compartment."

"Except me."

"What?"

"I have a gun in the glove compartment. Surely you didn't expect I would drive across this country, a vulnerable woman, without some sort of protection? I had a friend of mine drive into Vancouver and buy it, got it off some guy he knew.

It works. I fired it a couple times before I left. It was easy. I even hit the target a couple times."

"You have a gun in the glove compartment you've fired a couple of times and you think that's sensible? Oh, my God woman, are you out of your mind? What if I was some-kind of lunatic. Is it loaded?" He ripped the compartment open, pulling out the car manual, her gloves, a spare pair of sunglasses.

He stopped. Then turned to her, holding a bag of peanuts, pointing them at her, accusing.

"There is no gun is there?"

"Of course, not, this is Canada." She held back her laughter for a moment before exploding.

"Stop laughing, oh my God, I thought I was going to have to make a citizen's arrest. I'm only used to making police arrests. What if I screwed it all up?" He stuffed her belongings back into the little drawer and flipped it shut saying, "man I must have been a horrible cop, I can't even tell when you're kidding."

"Yeah, you're bad. I think it's good you got out when you did," she kidded.

"For the safety of the nation!" He laughed as hard as she did. "I'm going to get you back for that, I owe you for several pranks now. You do know that right?"

"I look forward to it Constable Han Solo," Charley quipped.

Chapter 13

The car motor and the air conditioner's soft hum were the only sounds in the red Ford for quite a while as they headed east again.

"Does it make you feel less significant or more after seeing all of that?" Charley finally broke the silence.

"You do ask the best questions," he said, smiling, "and less. The expanse of time the earth has been under development, the idea we live for such a brief teensy speck of that time, makes me feel like anything I do has no meaning or purpose whatsoever."

He squeezed his right fore-finger and thumb together until they touched to indicate what he meant by teensy.

"I feel that too." They were heading to Edmonton, having not long left the dinosaur museum at Drumheller, Alberta.

"But I also feel like we're privileged," Charley said. "What if we exist in the only time in history with this major technology and innovation, what if we destroy ourselves tomorrow, the Americans are under the thumb of a mad-man, and he's under the thumb of a lunatic in Russia, we could have every single piece of innovation ever created destroyed by these idiots with no record. Yet we got to live it. And we got to live it here." She waved her hand over the steering wheel indicating the country before her.

"I feel like I should keep this in a lead box." He indicated the notebook he had been writing things in along the way. As the only record of civilization remaining in some distant millions of years?"

"Except there will be no one to read it," Charley reminded him.

"Until a new species evolves."

"That can read English?"

"Shut up!" Damn her logic. He laughed, then continued. "I enjoyed the tour though. Do you believe in time travel?"

"Hell yeah, I mean right now it's the future at Nan's."

"That's not wrong."

"You like science fiction Han Solo?"

"I do, even though I haven't seen Star Wars, I love it. I think I'm contrary on the Star Wars thing now. I read it and write it in my spare time. I even started a trilogy but it needs work and I lost interest."

"Wow, you write? I write erotic romance." She stared straight ahead, face serious.

"You absolutely do not. I'm starting to figure you out now. You throw out these shocking things and I fall for them. Not falling for this one."

"Ooo-kay," she smiled and winked. She did write sexy romance books under the pen name CA Rose. They were quite popular. She'd used her writing to explore her sensual side, the part of herself that terrified her most.

"Stop, not falling for it. So, should I shut up or should we talk?"

"I don't mind if we talk, maybe you can tell me some more Mountie stories?"

"No, I think I told you enough on the drive, you know every place I've lived, every girl I dated and now you know I dabble in writing, it's your turn."

"Well, I was raised in Lewisporte, Dad worked with CN and Mom worked at Riffs. Mom's from there. I went to Nan's on Change Islands in the summer. I got an education degree at MUN, I taught in Wesleyville, got married, got divorced,

97

moved to BC, upgraded and got a job on Bowen Island. Parents both gone. That's it. I'm pretty boring."

"Mine too, both gone. So, you've lived in bookend islands." He felt connected to her in their mutual sadness at being parentless.

"Yep, but Newfoundland and Bowen Island are completely different."

"When was the last time you went home?"

"I haven't been back since I left."

"What? I only lived there four years and I've been back a few times, not in recent years but a few times."

"My parents passed away before I left, I fly Nan out here every year. It's easier to stay away."

"I've never met a Newfoundlander who lived somewhere else who didn't spend all their time figuring out how to get back home. My parents even moved back after many years away."

"I've wanted to but it was better to hang around Vancouver area. I've built a life for myself out there."

"A life with no friends."

"That's not fair. I built the life that works for me. I'm quite content."

"Content? Are you happy?"

"I'm happy enough. I do what makes me happy. I'm free, I have an income, I love my work and the kids I teach. I own my house outright, I hike, I have my Facebook page and blog and other writing as a hobby and I have a pension to look forward to not long down the road. Yeah, I guess I'm happy."

"Don't you know when you're happy? Is guessing enough?"

"What's with all the deep questions. Are you happy?" she tossed back at him.

"No, I'm not. I have had a good life, I liked the force and thought I didn't want more. But I did think I'd have a wife, a family but somehow that never worked out for me. As much as I loved my work, and I did, I enjoyed every moment, it is gone and I'm left all alone and unlike you, I don't like being alone. The RCMP is a lifestyle and I miss it. I miss them, my co-workers. They're still there but it's not the same . I feel their discomfort with me, with it—how it all happened."

"Maybe because you were forced into the retirement and didn't choose it?"

"Maybe, but I want to be happy. That's why I want to go home to Nan's for a while. It's quiet there, I can figure out what I'm going to do, what steps will make me happy. Living there might be the way to do it."

"That's partly what this trip is about for me I suppose, yeah, you're right I guess. I am not quite happy. I like my life but there is something missing. Maybe I'm trying to figure out what that is. Unlike you, I never wanted children. I'm not the maternal type. I don't even have a cat. I manage to keep my plants alive now that I have a thing on a timer that reminds me to water them."

"There is something you're not telling me."

"There is a lot I'm not telling you. My shit's my shit. Yours is yours. Let's just drive along and not get too heavy."

"Well I only wanted to know your favourite colour and your favourite movie, stuff like that."

"Yellow and Dirty Dancing."

"Really? Dirty Dancing? I was expecting you to say some Oscar-winning, deeply profound, boring thing like The English Patient."

"I like Forrest Gump? Something like that?"

"Exactly. That is a fantastic movie, watched it many times."

"Life is like a box of chocolates." She pronounced it 'choc-lits,' with an exaggerated southern USA accent

"And I often get the crappy orange piece," he whined.

"Pot of Gold, not Quality Street, right?"

"Always the cheap fucking Pot of Gold never the good stuff! That's my life."

"I want the good stuff, too, I want Quality Street, I want to be happy!" Charley raised her left fist to the sky. "Once, just once, I want a big purple piece!" She banged her hand on the wheel in pretend frustration.

"I'd love to give you a big purple piece," Garry offered in a perfect Forrest Gump voice. "Jinny always liked when I gave *her* a big purple piece, Mama always said, Forrest you gotta be a good boy and share your choc-lits, and I always done what mama said." He raised his eyebrows, wriggling them.

"Chocolate—I just want chocolate. Jeez. Settle down Indiana Jones." Charley squirmed at his off-colour joke.

"I like my hat," he said and changed the topic, referring to the hat she had bought him in Calgary, before they headed to Drumheller. It resembled the one Indiana Jones wore in the movies.

"Suits you," she smiled at him before looking back at the road ahead of her. He had been harmless in his joking and it had excited her to flirt. Plus, he was a good-looking guy and she was drawn to him, physically attracted.

Maybe she wasn't just talking about choc-lit at all.

Chapter 14

"I think it's cheaper to get a room with two Queen beds than a suite." Charley couldn't believe she had said that. But she was determined to defeat this fear of hers. If she had the same anxiety again she would call her old therapist and see how to handle it. She did not want to be afraid anymore. If she had to be ordinary in something, this was what she'd like it to be. She was calm now. But later tonight it might be different. She had to know. She could always let him drive if she had another restless, horrible sleep.

"Are you okay with that?" Garrison had no doubt about his attraction for her but even though he joked with her, he also knew that more than a joke was off limits. This wasn't about sleeping together but it wasn't about saving money either. They both had plenty of that. She had something to prove. Trust? He didn't know but he knew she could trust him. He was aware she had not slept well the first night in the Hostel but she had asked and so he decided to just go along if she was sure.

"Yeah, you seem harmless enough and you want a ride all the way home so you'll behave."

"It's about thirty bucks cheaper, yeah."

"Well then let's do it."

"Yeah?"

"And by it, I mean book two beds, one room. If it definitely costs less than two rooms can you book it? I'll do the next few. I think we're pretty on par for expenses so far."

"Except you're buying all the gas." Garrison had offered every single time. He purchased coffee and a couple of meals but she wouldn't let him pay for the gas.

"I told you why."

"Because you were gonna drive anyway, blah blah."

"Yes. Now shut up."

"Two nights?"

"Yeah, and book a night at Lloydminster also, I want to tour around up there a bit. So far, we've been to cities. No, let's find a small town somewhere between Lloydminster and Regina, a place where people don't go often. A prairie town.

"Oh yeah, that'll be good. So, one room, two Queen beds are booked. I'll do the others too." He punched an address into the navigation system and she watched as it calibrated the route.

"We're close to Edmonton already? Do you want to eat first or wait?"

"I'll have some chips and a coke for now? You want your Dr. Pepper?" He pulled up the bag from the floor in front of him.

"Set the chips in the middle." We're like a couple, taking care of each other, she thought.

"Kay." He booked the room somewhere past Lloydminster and hit confirm. There was no way she was going to reimburse him for this. This should make up for her insistence on paying the gas across Canada. He had been jotting down the amount on the gas pumps and would keep a tally. He wasn't worried about money, he had a regular pension, finally, after a bureaucratic battle, a decent amount in savings and zero bills. He was lucky and he knew it. He was enjoying this trip quite a bit. He flipped open the journal he was keeping. And re-read what he had written earlier.

"Went to Drumheller which has the Royal Tyrrell Museum. Charlotte bought me a hat in Calgary as a joke. She cracks me up, keeps me on my toes. But it was a kind thing. It is kind of like what Indiana Jones would wear so I put on a white shirt, khaki shorts and wore it the entire time we were in the museum. Nobody noticed. I guess this outfit isn't so unusual to the people who visit

dinosaur museums. Or, perhaps they're all too polite to tell me I look ridiculous."

At some point his writing had gone from bullet points to narration. He jotted down the amount of the hotel rooms and then forwarded the reservation information to Charlotte's number. They checked in less than an hour later and Charlotte threw herself on the bed.

"Tired?"

"Lazy. I know I should get out there, do stuff but I don't think I will."

"I can get out of your hair if you want to sleep?"

"You don't mind? It's half your room."

"I can entertain myself. I'll grab a cab and go sightseeing. Text me when you wake up."

"Thanks."

Garry unpacked a few things, popped his wallet in his pocket and waved as he went out the door. Charley made her way to the bathroom and turned on the water to fill the tub. Her back was aching from the driving. And she needed to think.

She sank into the clear water, leaned her head on the edge of the tub and sighed. This trip had been about meeting people along the way but because she had a companion she hadn't done so. That needed to change. Perhaps people would chat to her if she did stuff alone. A single woman was approachable. With a man at her side nobody started conversations. They had been sitting at tables and walking through public places for days now and the only conversation she had had with a stranger was the one with Patsy, the bigot. She sat straight up. She could test this right now. He had gone somewhere on his own, she could do the same.

She hauled herself up out by the bar on the wall. Damn, her back was still sore. She did need exercise. A walk would do her some good. She wrapped herself in a robe and peered out the window.

"Damn, fuck. Not fit to walk." The rain poured into large puddles, the sky dark and eerie, showing no signs of clearing up.

The mall!

Dressed in a pair of leggings, a red and white comfy tunic, and a pair of running shoes, she dashed to the van cursing herself for not bringing rain gear into her room. Damp, she started the engine and set off.

The West Edmonton Mall is the tenth largest in the world. Charley ordered everything she could online so malls didn't interest her generally but the sheer size of it would allow for a good long stroll and she could people watch and maybe eat alone. Or she could sidle up on a barstool somewhere and chat somebody up.

She had heard about the place but entering it was a whole other thing. It wasn't merely a mall, it was an experience. She supposed she'd known there was an amusement park inside, but had forgotten.

She loved rides and Galaxy-Land boasted the world's largest indoor Roller Coaster the Mindbender and she'd be damned if she wasn't going on that thing. She paid, excited with anticipation.

It wasn't as busy as expected, since it was mid-week and close to supper time. She meandered, looking at the rides before deciding to first try the Galaxy Orbiter that twirled, dipped and thrilled riders all through the entire park.

A middle-aged woman and four teens were ahead of her. Because the trains were set so four were in a carriage, the woman sat beside her, ashen-faced, post-ride regret already set.

"Dear Lord don't let me get sick," she said.

"Dear Lord don't let me fall out," Charley replied, eyes sparkling.

"Oh, my God that can't happen, can it?" The terrified woman appeared set to bolt.

"Nah, I'm kidding. At least I don't think it can." No point in giving false hope. Part of the thrill was the idea something bad could happen.

"I hate this kind of thing. Hate, hate, hate it. Well, I've never been on one before but I know I hate it."

"A roller coaster virgin! Then, why do it?"

"Because the kids dared me. I know, I know. Sometimes you have to break out of your rut though, try new things." She shrugged and offered a wry smile.

"That I understand. You know you could get out, live with the shame forever. Or you could hang on and go!"

"That's my choice uh? Everlasting shame or certain death, " the woman, who introduced herself as Nicole, said.

"It's not *certain* you're not going to die and I'm Charley," she replied in a tone that implied they likely would.

"I may die of a heart attack." Nicole placed her hand on her chest.

"If you have heart problems you're not supposed to ride these things ."

Two teenage boys were strapping themselves into their carriage, all gangly arms and pimples, one with a swoosh side-bang haircut he kept flipping and allowing to fall back down over his left eye.

"Well we'll see if I do now I suppose. You're not afraid Charley?" she asked.

"Terrified but I love it. It's a thrill." She couldn't explain why she loved it so much. Her palms were sweaty, there was an overwhelming urge to jump out and run, yet she was excited too.

"Guess I'm facing my fears." The woman let out a little screech as the train started moving. The two boys facing them raised their arms, ready.

Charley did the same, in solidarity, letting out a big, "woohoo!"

"Woohoo," Nicole grinned, raising her arms also. "Guess I better hang on and go."

With that the ride accelerated, screams and screeches lost in the rattle of wheels on steel and the terrified shrieks and wails of other riders. Charley closed her eyes, enjoying the sensation of being out of control, the idea of the choice between shame and the fear of death, swirling in her brain like the roller coaster twisting through the air. She needed to find a center space, a location between them. Fear and shame. Those were the two things that had kept her out of life for a long time. But death had never been certain, though she had used the fear of it to hide her shame for far too long. When the ride stopped, tears streamed down her face and the lady next to her touched her hand.

"You were afraid, weren't you? I thought you were so brave," Nicole said, her voice kind.

"I'm going to try to not be afraid anymore," Charley replied." She wiped a hand across her face, drying her cheeks.

"I think that was so fun! Yeah, it was terrifying too but I guess you should try the terrifying things at times, you should do them because it might be the most fun you ever had! I think I'd do it again!" the woman laughed.

"I think it was very worthwhile and I'd definitely do it again," Charley replied, her head cleared by the experience. There were other things she wanted to try, things that had terrified her for a long time that might be fun. Being so out of control, having no real grasp on her destiny, even for a few short moments had been cathartic.

She stepped off the little train and bid farewell to the kind lady who had shared her weak moments and fussed over her emotional breakdown. How sweet she was.

As Charley walked away she pulled out her phone and sent a text to Garry.

Hey, I had a bath and wasn't tired anymore. I'm at the amusement park at the West Edmonton Mall, want to come by for a few rides and have some supper?

His reply was immediate.

I'm over by the sea lions, I'll be there shortly. I love a roller coaster.

She replied. She decided to be honest.

I'm terrified on them, maybe you can hold my hand. I need a friend.

The smiley emoticon he sent back put a little flip in her stomach and she walked to the line-up for the Mind Bender and waited for him to show up.

Chapter 15

"If I keep eating like this they're going to charge me commercial rates at North Sydney to cross the gulf." Garry rubbed his flat belly, grabbed the remote and flicked on the television.

"Go on, we walked every bit of it off in the mall. That place is pretty cool, maybe tomorrow we'll go to the water park if it's raining."

"Maybe. What would you like to watch? I'm going to shower." He tossed her the remote, pulled off his shirt and sat on the bed removing his shoes and socks.

Charley picked it up. She watched him undressing, caught herself and looked away.

She should sleep with him right now, tonight, get it out of the way. It had been long enough, healing must surely happen after all this time. A casual encounter with a nice man, on a road trip would be normal, it might even be good. *If she were normal. If she were good.* Her thoughts drifted for a second to the last time she'd been intimate, if you could call it that. Charley shook her head, as though it were an Etch-a-Sketch, bringing herself back to the present. Thinking about the past never resolved things. She had thought far too much about it for a long time. It was when she chose not to things got better. She shivered a little when she heard the water turn off and had her pajamas and robe ready when he came out.

"My turn," she averted her eyes as she went past him to the bathroom, then spoke, "Do you mind if I take the bed closest to the bathroom, I sometimes have to get up at night, reduces the chance of me waking you." It was also the bed nearest the door.

"Sure," he agreed and he picked his bag up and transferred it over to the bed near the window.

Garry watched her disappear into the bathroom, pondering. Charley tried not to be attractive, or rather, she didn't do anything to accentuate her looks. But she was, nonetheless. He dropped his towel and changed into a pair of plaid pajama bottoms, the sounds of her bathroom routine muffled by the television. He flicked through the channels, hovering over the scrambled porn for a moment before moving on to a renovation show.

When his phone vibrated he grabbed it before a second notification could come through.

"Hi Nan," he answered. Her voice would be a welcome detour from the direction his thoughts had headed.

"You in Edmonton yet?" Geraldine didn't bother with hello.

"Got here earlier, just in the room a short while ago, we went to the mall. Staying for two nights now."

"Oh good, I worries you know. I knows you said you would call the once but I figured it's late here and if you called too late the phone would wake me up." It never would. Ger was deaf and turned her hearing aid off at night. She just needed to know.

"I know Nan, I forgot about the time difference again. I should have called from the mall." It wasn't true. He had not remembered to call at all. "You can call me anytime though, I'm not driving and I can answer if we have service. We have had a few down spots but it's fine."

"How are you and Charley getting on?"

"Best kind, she is in the bathroom now," he said, then scrunched his face up. Damn, what had he done?

"What? You're in the same room. With Charley?" Her voice wasn't scandalized, or upset, it was angry.

"Nan, we have two beds. Nothing is going on."

"Nothing better go on. I told her grandmother you were a gentleman, and after what that girl has been through she don't need no trouble from you. You keep away from her, don't lay a hand on her."

"What? What do you mean?" What the hell had Charley been through? Charley's entry into the room prevented him from asking.

"Don't worry Nan, everything is alright here. We are safe and sound, Charley is out from the bathroom. I should go, she might want to get to sleep."

"Okay but you mind what I said," Ger's voice was quiet, " and it's not that I don't trust you, you've always been a good boy, grew up to be a good man. And I know you have had your own troubles lately but you need to be nice to Charley. Respectful. It was hard to get her grandmother to even ask if you could get a ride, and with good reason. Don't take advantage of her kindness okay?"

"You don't have to worry Nan. We'll be careful." He smiled at Charley.

"Good night Nan, I love you." He clicked his phone off, all previous thoughts of Charlotte's attractiveness replaced with curiosity and concern for her.

"You told your grandmother we were sharing a room?" Peeved, Charlotte flicked the volume down on the television. There would be speculation though that was happening regardless. God knows people loved to talk about her.

"By accident."

"By accident uh? I want to be clear. Suggesting we share a room in no way suggests we do anything but share the room. Yours, mine." She indicated the two beds. If something were to happen, it would be on her terms.

"I understand that. You have my word. I won't bother you." As much as he didn't like being scolded, he needed her to know he understood and would respect her boundaries.

"Good." She breathed, then sighed, shook her head and sat on her bed.

"What?"

"It's just, I'm stupid. I, when I suggested we share a room, I kind of thought perhaps it might lead to—I'm trying to get over my past and well, I'm not good at this honesty stuff but I'm not good at games either."

"You thought it would lead to more?" Garry hadn't seen that confession coming. He could have sworn she was terrorized the last time they spent the night together.

"I don't know. I was hoping I'd recovered enough. I don't know if I want to go into details but let's just say, I had a trauma. A big one, with a man. And I haven't shared a room with one since I moved away from home. Hell, I haven't shared a room with a girlfriend. I was trying to be normal but I'm just not normal."

She said all the words without emotion, her voice flat, the enormity of it hitting her after she said them. She had not even said these things to her therapists, years-ago.

"I'm not sure what to say but I'm willing to listen." If there was anything he had learned since his issues had arisen was that a supportive ear was usually what people needed most.

"Garry, I'm not normal. I can't get close to people, I can't talk to them, tell them what I'm feeling, ask for help. The last one, that's a big one. I hug people when I greet them but I don't feel fondness towards people and give sincere hugs, except for Nan. And men, well, I've never been alone in a room with a man, until we were alone in the hostel, and to be honest, I don't even know if I've been alone in a car with a man since—"

"— and then your Nan forced me on you." That appeared cruel and didn't sound like something she would do.

"I know it seems mean but I also know she must have trusted you to do this. Nan might even prefer if we hooked up, like normal people do because I've been absent from real life for so long."

"I suppose." Absent from life. That was an apt description of his past five years. "I'm not going to ask you what happened but I am going to tell you that you don't have to worry about me. I will not bother you."

"You already bother me." She was still monotone.

"I can book another room. It's fine."

"No. Stay. God, I hate all this seriousness but I guess this is just a serious thing." She looked up, her smile faint. Her fingers twirled, tracing the pattern on the bedspread.

"Are you sure?"

"Yes. Um, there is something I haven't done in a long while I am going to do, and no, it's not that." She breathed in deeply before speaking again. "I need your help."

"How can I help you? What do you want me to do?" Garry could have sworn this woman didn't need help with anything on earth. But she wasn't tough. She was vulnerable. At least right in this moment she was.

"Nothing. I did it. I just faced what I was most afraid of."

"You did what? I'm sorry Charley, I'm trying to understand but you've lost me." Did she want his help or not?

"I asked for help. What I have been most afraid of doing is asking for help and I asked you for it. I know, I told you I'm not normal."

"So, you don't want help, you wanted to ask?"

"No, I do need help, but asking you for it was the first step," Her voice held some of its usual tone now.

"So, you don't need my help at-the-moment, you only need to know I'm available for when you want help? And you aren't good at asking for help so you decided to ask me so you could overcome your fear of asking for help?"

"Something like that yeah. God, I hate all this—I don't know, drama." Their eyes met.

He turned his back breaking the eye contact.

He replied, his voice abrupt. "I think I'm going to have to say no. I'm sorry but you can't use me as a practice board for your neurosis. It's not fair. You know I've been through stuff too, I have my own problems. I can't be expected to be on call for when you need help. Do I look like Doctor freakin' Phil to you?" He arranged his face into a serious expression and turned to stare straight at her.

"I'm sorry, I didn't think, I mean, I'm trying to…" she was deflated, and he couldn't continue.

"Would you look at your face!" He glanced away, afraid he would laugh but needing to stay serious, searching for the words. "Of course anything you need Charley, I'm sure you're as normal as can be under there somewhere but if you need to bawl or scream or be crazy or cry or whatever I'll do what I can to help you through. Or share a room and keep to my own side so you can feel safe with people. Whatever you—" He turned back to her.

Wooomph!

He stumbled from the impact of a huge pillow hurled from the adjacent bed. Charley was standing there with a face registering something between delight and anger.

He picked up another pillow and made his way towards her, whacking her hard and she picked up another and tried to hit him back, their laughter filling the room as they sparred, both winding up on a bed, together.

Then in moment of silence their eyes met. They stared at each other for a long moment, the room quiet and Garry reached out and stroked her hair back over her forehead, making way for his lips to brush across it in a brief kiss.

"Let's watch Holmes on Homes k?" He shifted up, putting a pillow behind his head, to prop himself up on her bed. Then he motioned for her to come up and sit beside him. She didn't hesitate, grabbing the pillows and arranging it so they were sitting together in companionable silence. Her fingers crept down and gave his warm hand a grateful squeeze and he squeezed back and didn't let go.

Mike's indignant voice blared from the television right before he ripped out the walls and ceiling in a basement he hadn't planned on having to reconstruct.

"I like this show," Charley commented.

"I know, me too. Plus, Mike's right. Sometimes things need to be torn down, ripped all to shreds, so you can start all over. Before you can *make it right*." Garry used the popular television star's catch phrase, and knew it was corny. Charley knew it too.

She smiled. Sometimes corny was just the normal that was required.

Chapter 16

Even though the sun shone bright the following day and they could do anything they wanted outside, Charley and Garry went back to the mall. They splashed and played at the waterpark, having a blast, along with many other mall-goers.

After, dried-off and lazy, they located a laundromat and did laundry, reading in companionable silence as their clothing tumbled together in the machines. Then, basking in the mundane they strolled around a bit, ate a picnic lunch, and went window shopping.

"This feels like a date; can we call it a date? I'll take you to a movie after dinner," asked Garry on the way to a pizza place.

"I don't think so. My date requirements are much higher. Like, fancy higher. Hoity-toity higher.

Let's go on a date one day though. A real one. Ask me. And we'll make arrangements."

"OK, would you go on a date with me?" Garry politely inquired. "You know I've never asked for a first date. I've always met people through friends."

"I'm sorry, I'm seeing somebody," Charley skipped away, towards the pizza place.

"I'm crushed." Garry chased her. Catching up he asked, "who is he? Is it somebody I know?"

"You'll live, but just friends though for now but I might date him. He's a big guy, a Mountie." She made gestures with her hands to indicate his size.

"Asshole, I hate cops. I can take him. When I see him I'll—"

"Quebec City." Charley stated.

"Uh? What about it?"

"We'll go on a date there. It could be romantic. Plus, I said before remember, at dinner in Calgary. I should know you well enough by then to see if I want to date you."

"Oh, you want to. But I'll take it. Quebec City we have a date. It'll be very fancy. I'll take care of everything. And so, you know, Quebec City is *just* Quebec in Quebec City." He winked.

"I knew that. So, cool, a date." She drew out the word cool so it sounded coo-well. "Whatever shall I wear?" She fanned herself Scarlett O'Hara style.

"It'll be semi-formal. You need to wear a dress and heels. Not, red and white. Do you own that kind of thing?"

"Fuck no."

"Well you're going to have to buy stuff. I recommend you go all out. Hair, makeup, the entire thing. I've got a suit with me. This is my first ever real big date you know, well except for taking Lorraine Jenkins to grad. But she's a second cousin so that doesn't count."

"I don't think I've had a big, formal, first date since grad either. I mean, I married so young and then after, well…"

"I can't imagine you married."

"No?" Why did that sting? Did he think nobody would want her? "Yeah, it was a disaster." She shut it down, they were walking into the pizza place.

"You're just so independent." He undid the sting with his words.

"And you'll do all the parley vous-ing?" she asked, changing the subject. She would not discuss the past with him.

"Je serai ravi de faire tous le discours sur notre date!"

"Wow, that's sexy. French me some more."

"Not in public!" He feigned shock. "But after our date in Quebec I'll be happy to français vous toute la nuit."

"I have a strong desire to say *Oui* to that, even though I haven't the foggiest idea what you said."

"*I'd* say *Oui* to it," the hostess quipped giving Garry an appreciative look that started somewhere above his knees and ended at his eyes.

"Parlez-vous français?" Garry asked the lovely blond girl who appeared to be in her twenties.

"Oui, je suis originaire de France, près de Naples. Je suis arrivé au Canada quand j'avais deux ans avec mes parents."

"J'ai voyagé à Naples il y a quinze ans, c'était magnifique…ouch!"

"Come on, back to Edmonton," Charley admonished Garry, and to the hostess she said, "we'll take a table for two." She smacked him on the arm.

"God woman, it's not like we're on a date," Garry grinned, rubbing it. Had she been a tad jealous? He like to practice his French when the opportunity arose.

"And we won't if you keep flirting with young blondes. Shit that sounds petty, doesn't it?"

"Yeah, it is. I love it. You're jealous!"

"Am not!" Maybe she was. Damn.

"You're jealous, you're jealous," he sang, taunting her.

"Fuck off, Let's get pizza."

Heather, the hostess, raised an eyebrow at the couple unsure of what to make of their teasing. The man was a nice tall drink of lemonade though, and the girl with him was a bit plain but it seemed as if he liked her so, whatever. She led them to their table.

"Your waitress will be here shortly to take your drink order." She walked away swaying her hips a bit more than was natural.

"I'm not jealous," Charley repeated.

"Suuuure you're not. Hey, I understand, all of this," he gestured his two hands down his body, "is far too much for the ladies to resist."

"There are buses to North Sydney from Edmonton," the waitress stopped by with an iPad, "where is the nearest bus station?" Charley inquired.

"No need to be hasty now," Garry said, with a grin. It was rare he had the upper hand with Charley so he was enjoying it, perhaps too much.

"I apologize, don't know, I'm Wendy, I'm your waitress."

"Do you speak French? Ouch!" Garry jumped when Charley kicked him under the table.

"No but Heather does, if you would rather order in French I can get her?" The waitress was as mystified as the hostess by this couple.

"We speak perfectly good English," Charley informed her.

"Oh, ok, well what can I get you to drink?" She tapped the iPad again.

"I'll have a glass of wine, something red and French," Garry said, straight-faced.

Charlotte shot looks like daggers at him before ordering a beer.

"They have a *French*-Canadian Pizza," he declared, staring at the menu.

"Stop it." Charley ordered.

"Come on. Let me have some fun. I can't remember the last time a beautiful woman was jealous over me."

"I'm not jealous over you." Gah, she wanted to throw her beer on him. She took a long swig instead.

"What then?" She didn't seem the jealous type so perhaps there was something real here. He caught her eye, sincerity in the question.

"Well, let's order first."

The waitress took the orders and left. Their drinks were on the table moments later.

"Spill it, why the jealousy?" He sipped his wine. "I should have gotten a beer, that's what I get for teasing you. So, what rubbed you the wrong way about our lovely hostess?"

"Nothing. It's, well, I used to be like that you know? I was flirty and young and while it got me in a lot of trouble, I don't know, when I see girls like that, I kind of get jealous of it. I miss the young, happy-go-lucky girl I was before, um, before I had to grow up."

"Makes sense."

"Does it? It's not childish?"

"Yeah, it's childish. But it's also common. I miss who I was too, before I got injured. It changed me. I think now, after all this time it might have been for the better but sometimes, I want to —"

"Hop on a plane and fly home?"

"Hop on a plane and fly anywhere."

"You'll tell me someday." He would. He was being very patient with her, she'd return the favour.

"Yes, I will, but not in a pizza place in Edmonton."

"And not in Quebec City, you can't be ruining our date with deep dark confessions."

"Deal."

And he leaned aside to allow their waitress to drop a steaming pizza on their table. They each grabbed a piece.

"I never thought I would say it but I could live in this mall." Charley blew on her fingers; the pizza was hot.

"I know! It's wicked. But Lloydminster is next. I don't know anything about that city. Why did you want to go there? Any particular reason?"

"Oh, it's a cool thing, the reason I want to go. It has a quirk. I can't wait to show you why it's unique. Don't Google, let it be a surprise!"

"Deal." He gestured to the waitress who came right over.

"Can I get a Molson Canadian please? Wine just doesn't quite go with pizza."

"Tell it to the Italians," Charlie quipped as she blew on a slice and chewed down into it, rolling her eyes at its deliciousness before launching a discussion on what movie they would see after their dinner.

Chapter 17

Charley popped the baseball hat with its red maple leaf on her head, then double-checked the description she had written for her broadcast. Making sure her index cards were in order she took a breath and tapped the screen at ten local, the time she'd chosen hoping it would reach the most people. The short video would be saved and shared but she liked to get as many live online while she streamed. She loved the comments even if some of them pointed out all the problems in the country rather than the positives.

"Good evening everybody," Charley began, "I hope you're all doing well. I'm here in Edmonton, ready to head out tomorrow and our trip has been smooth and uneventful. My companion has been generous with helping me figure out what to talk about as we travel. One thing I want to talk to you about today are the places we have been but also about some of the places we won't be able to get to.

We spent some time at Drumheller, checking out the dinosaur museum there and we had a great discussion about how it made us feel to have the reality before us that the universe and existence itself is so much larger than our human brains can grasp. That was a deep topic and it got me thinking that even this country is a bigger place than our brains can grasp. It's going to take weeks to drive straight across but we're also forty-six hundred kilometers from North to south. I've been thinking about the vastness of our geography as well as the largeness of our diversity, with the majority of our people originally coming from places outside of Canada.

This week I had a truly disturbing conversation with a person who embodied all the negativity in Canada, in one brief chat. This person was angry, entitled, prejudiced and unaware she was either of those things. I didn't engage with the person, perhaps shocked by such ignorance, since I rarely ever encounter it anymore. But if we're going to talk about diversity, we should include people like that. We're diverse not only in terms of culture but in terms of our opinions on culture.

Even in these past few days some of the idealism I had when setting out on this trip has been crinkled a bit, not only by this but by the fact I'm missing out on so much, and feel I'm misrepresenting things. So, I want to be clear, I'm going through Canada but to fairly represent I need to go *about* Canada a lot more than I am. This one trip won't tell the entire story. Or even many of the stories. It'll tell just a tiny story, mine and the few people I meet along the way."

This was her most preachy broadcast yet and she needed to lighten it up. But her next topic was serious too.

"I should tell you about my ride on the roller coaster yesterday at the West Edmonton Mall where I met a wonderful lady who decided to take the ride with a group of teenagers. I was alone and even though I'm scared to death of these rides I also love them, there is something so exhilarating and healing about being out of control for a short while. So, there we were, two strangers, strapped into this contraption for the sole purpose of being hurled through space for thrills. When it was over, I found myself quite emotional, the ride somehow cathartic, a liberating experience that moved me to tears. This perfect stranger reached out and consoled me, even though at the beginning of the ride it was her expressing fear.

After our little adventure, we went our separate ways. But I'll never forget how, in a moment in time, we were there for each other. I, for her, at the beginning of the journey, her for me, at the end.

It was fleeting, it was significant. Perhaps that's a commentary on Canadian life right there. It might be a human thing, this sort of compassion, but we in this country have the freedom to practice it frequently due to our unprecedented peace. To reach out, console and provide solace to a person because they need it in that moment is a good thing, and a common thing, and not an insignificant thing.

Yeah, I guess I'm in a deep and introspective place today, I promise I'll find more fun and lighthearted topics as we go along.

Have a great evening everybody. I'm about to write a blog post so watch for that and sign up to get it delivered directly to your email at the address below. Thank you and this is *Charley through Canada* signing out."

Charley clicked the button and sighed. Yep, just too serious. She was not feeling particularly inspired and hoped this changed as she moved through the country. The people watching would need more and better. She pulled up the blog to start writing, her topic, how boring and awful her broadcasts were. A little self-deprecation always made for fun reading.

She added a dozen photos and hit publish before shutting down. She picked up her phone immediately to text Garry to return. Then she stopped.

Why am I in such a hurry to have him back here? She thought. I like being alone. She put the phone down again, picked up the remote control, flicking on the television. She scrolled for five minutes then hit click and turned it back off.

What the hell, she could be alone when she had to be. Right now, she was bored. She sent the text.

She wasn't being needy, she was enjoying his company she told herself.

The little blip of excitement she felt when she heard his key in the hotel room door indicated she was enjoying it a little bit more than she ought to.

Chapter 18

Somehow, they managed to get to the four 100-foot high red spires that indicated the quirk about Lloydminster without Garry knowing anything about it.

"It's the border? In the middle of the city?" Garry fingered the coat of arms of Alberta and Saskatchewan. "Wow, I can't believe I didn't know."

"I thought it would be fun to come here, see it. Be in both provinces at once. It's the fourth meridian of the Dominion Land Survey which was supposed to coincide with 110° west longitude but they screwed up and that's twenty meters or so that-away, I think." She pointed west with her hand.

"How do you know all this stuff?" He walked around eying the words Saskatchewan and Alberta that ran up the sides of the long markers.

"I have an advanced brain, highly evolved and quite clever enough to use Google," she responded, a grin on her face.

"Well it's pretty remarkable uh? You're right, it is a cool quirk."

"This is a nice town, I think it's a good representation of Alberta and Saskatchewan with a mix of the agriculture and the oil industry as big players in the economy and culture."

"But you think the oil industry should go, right?"

"It isn't a matter of if I should think it should, it will."

"And what would a place like this one do?"

"The same thing places like Newfoundland did when the salt-cod fishery died. Adjust. Times change Indiana Jones."

"It'll destroy the area."

"Really? Because there was an Alberta long before the oil sands were developed. Do you know the early indigenous people used the bitumen to seal up their canoes? There is a cool history there, before they started extracting the crude to sell. Then at another point, in the late fifties, they were going to use nuclear explosions to kind of liquefy the oil so it could be pumped out, but the government shut that down."

"You're serious?" Garry blinked, incredulous.

"Deadly serious. They didn't start extracting it until the late sixties if I recall what I read about it. And of course, the Cold Lake Oil Sands are partly in Saskatchewan so this province," she moved so she stood on the Saskatchewan side of the pole, "benefits directly."

"It's a good thing they didn't go the nuclear route."

"Agree. Good old Diefenbaker prevented that. So, they found another way and Lloydminster is benefiting from it. Of course, you can't drink alcohol here but otherwise it's a great town."

"What? What do you mean?" This news was more fascinating than the nuclear explosion bit.

"This town was started as a totally Utopian British settlement that had zero alcohol."

"And it still does? Now?" Garry was shocked.

"Oh yeah, well, the Saskatchewan side has alcohol, but not the Alberta side."

"That's crazy." He looked up and down the street.

"Yeah, it's also a big fat lie." Charley moved, she had to be swift to avoid the swat on the butt he tried to deliver.

"I have to learn to never believe a word you say." He shook his head, laughing.

"I have another place to show you. I saw it when I was reading a bit more about Lloydminster on Wikipedia. I think you'll like it." Come on, she led the way to the van.

They parked and walked towards the Lloydminster City Hall. The monument stood about two meters high and depicted a RCMP officer consoling a young boy crying over what appeared to be an injured dog. Cast in bronze the word HOPE was emblazoned across the front along with a Canadian Flag.

Garry approached the site, walking around, silent as he read the accompanying plaque, interpreting the work and its intended meaning for himself.

"It's nice, isn't it? A former local RCMP officer spearheaded the project. He died shortly after. I came across it by accident online and since you were in the force I thought you might like to see it." Charley smiled. She was pleased at herself for this.

"Hope," Garry spoke the word out loud. His eyes were red rimmed.

"Now don't go snottin' and bawlin'," Charley ordered in her best imitation of her grandmother.

Garry laughed, wiped his eyes and sniffed.

"I'm a bit of a sook, as they say down home. I guess I miss it you know. The force. It's more than a job, it's a life. I was a decent cop, the moving around was sometimes difficult but always interesting. The places I spent most of my career, we're not going to visit on this tour through the country. I was mostly up in the territories. It's a different life there. And it's amazing but I've also seen people who have more poverty and hardship than you can imagine, where there wasn't a snowflake in the tundra amount of hope. I've worked with people who could have had decent happy lives who turned to drugs and crime instead because they had not a shred of it."

Charley was taken aback as his tone altered. "I guess even a snowflake in a tundra is a flicker of hope, right?"

There was silence. Then he spoke. His voice was grave. It came from a different place far darker and colder than the present. Darker and colder than the northern nights in the places he served as a police officer all those many years.

"This country isn't all great Charley. And worse, it isn't even all good. In fact, some places are downright miserable. We can't be blind to that reality. There are places where people are committing suicide in large numbers, twelve-year old children are killing themselves. *Children*, Charlie. There is precious little hope in many of these communities and it's complex and sad and rooted in what we as a country did in the past."

Charley stood still, afraid to breathe. She wanted to ask what the solution was, what she could do to help. She wanted to erase the anguish in his face. She listened instead.

"A white cop, a white boy, a golden retriever. Do you think this actually represents Canadian reality? No, it represents the sanitized, idealized image we have, the CBC-scrubbed, nostalgia-filled, sugary-sweet drivel we are fed. What if it were an indigenous boy with his mother who had been murdered, being consoled by an officer? Because that's the kind of consoling I had to do in one place where I was stationed. I don't think we could wrap the word *hope* around that, do you?" He turned to her, "*Do you*?" His anger changed his features, hardened them. His eyes drilled into hers. She looked away.

"I don't know what to say. I thought it was a nice thing to see. I'm sorry."

"Oh damn, Charley, no it was a nice thought, that's not it. In fact, it's good you brought me here, this sort of anger needs a place to go. That's what my therapist says anyway." He swiped a hand through his hair, straightened his shoulders and took a breath.

Charley waited.

"It is a beautiful statue," he said, "and kudos to the gentleman who spearheaded its creation. It is a nice sentiment." He decided not to qualify it further. The man deserved honour for trying.

Charley took a deep breath. Then she spoke.

"I've been more than a little angry that we didn't know about the residential schools, for example. I am a well-read, educated person, a bit of a news junkie, and during my life there was never a thing mentioned about that in school, in university, in the media. I had no idea. And it angers me. I had a right to know. I don't know that I could have done anything but if I didn't know perhaps others didn't know either, people who *could* have done something, and maybe would have. It's only been in the past two or three years I've realized what sort of horror the people of our first nations endured—no, the horrors we imposed upon them. May as well lay the blame solely where it belongs and stop saying it as though it was some kind of act of nature."

"I don't know what to do about it Charley. I know I made mistakes, I judged people while policing them, because I didn't understand why they were the way they were. It's a selfish thing to have to be damaged yourself to get how people become damaged uh?"

"You think you're damaged?"

"Can you take a photo of me with this monument?" He handed her his iPhone, ignoring her question.

Surprised at the turnaround, Charley agreed. He glanced at the screen when she handed him the phone.

"Not every moment with me will be magical and pretty Charley, sometimes moments get wrecked. I'm often the person who wrecks them but I'm working on that. I'm sorry I didn't respond the way you expected when you brought me here." He gave the statue one more look and smiled. It was a good thing to do, he thought, even if he would have done it differently.

She handed him back his camera, still not speaking. She could not think of a single word to say.

Chapter 19

The young Charley would have scolded him for turning a nice gesture into a political rant. And as much as she wanted to recapture herself, maturation had happened and she wasn't the scolding type anymore. Plus, his wasn't just a political rant, it was a personal one. Something haunted him. Her grandmother had said he would tell her why he refused to fly. It all had to be connected.

He seemed to have this combination of missing being a police officer and a disdain for it. Or was the latter directed at himself. She had a tightness in her shoulders and her hands ached from holding the wheel. She breathed and let her shoulders fall, loosening her fingers. She split the tension open, dispersed it, with a change of topic.

"It's fucking flat, isn't it?"

"Yeah, it's fucking flat," Garry laughed and agreed. Embarrassed by his earlier tirade, he was grateful. They had only stopped once at a gas station, driving through Saskatoon and they were now on a highway known as Louis Riel Trail headed to Regina.

"I'm struck by the sky. There is so much of it. It goes on forever and the sun is different here also, there is something in the atmosphere that gives it an odd glow."

"What did you think of the bridges in Saskatoon? I had no idea what the city looked like so all of those bridges were a surprise to me."

"Yeah, I know. It was pretty. I must confess the only thing I knew about Saskatchewan was it was flat and they grow wheat. Oh, and it's a Trapezoid."

"Well this trip is about learning, right?"

"Are we learning anything? A short stop in this place, a quick stop in that one. How can we learn anything? It's like trying to experience sex by doing a lot of kissing."

"Kissing is fun too. Nothing wrong with a little making out," Garry kidded.

Charley glanced at him. He stared straight ahead, eyes on the road. He was a nice-looking man, slender like a runner, broad shouldered. He had a perfect smile, his face was unshaven, scruffy even, his wavy hair down to his collar. He wore the same type of thing every day, khaki shorts, a T-shirt, socks, running shoes and sunglasses. He only wore a hat in Drumheller, the one she had bought him.

"I don't know what to make of you." She knew she sounded like her grandmother.

"I don't even know what that means." He looked at her, the expression unfamiliar.

"It means I don't understand you."

"Well I don't understand you either."

"I'm trying."

"I'm not. I'm not trying to understand you. I'm trying to *be* understanding though."

"See, that right there. Who says things like that?"

"Me? I mean, if you want to explain yourself to me that's fine, but it's not mandatory. People are who they are right? You can be understanding of that without understanding their underlying motivation."

"This isn't a normal conversation. Average, ordinary people don't talk like this."

"I can't believe you confused us with average, ordinary people." Garry lifted his glasses, then said, "I could eat soon."

"We're not ordinary or average? Sure, we are? There is a town ahead, Dundurn. I figured we could stay there for the night."

"No, we are definitely different. There is a military base there. I considered joining the military before I decided on the RCMP."

"Really? A military base? Can we go there?" Charley was fascinated.

"No, they'll shoot you on sight."

She stuck out her tongue at his lie.

"So, we're not ordinary? Not average?" she asked.

"No, we are weird. Completely weird. There is a hotel, oh and a restaurant called Kathy's Restaurant and Motel on Willms St."

"Let's go there." She needed food too.

Garry punched it into the navigation system and they were there in under five minutes. It was a nondescript building and most definitely closed.

"Okay, so on to the next option."

After a short drive, they arrived and were delighted The Little Wok Restaurant was open. They were seated and had their food in short order.

"This is good." Charley poked her fork into her Pork Noodle Bowl.

"The curried Chicken is fantastic also." Garry offered her a taste and she stuck her fork in a piece of his food, motioning for him to try a piece of pork.

"That *is* good." She restarted their earlier conversation asking him, "why don't you think we're ordinary? Average?"

"Well, aside from the fact there isn't anyone who is ordinary or average if people were true to themselves, let me spell out why we're unusual."

"Shoot." She sipped her water, lips pursed around the straw, eyes up starting at his, waiting.

"You are fairly ordinary. As am I. We have a lot of ordinary parts. A cop, a teacher, nothing unusual or special about that."

"But you said we weren't ordinary. Now you say we are? Jeez." She lifted her water glass, removed the straw and sucked a piece of ice out of it.

"No, I didn't, I said, *we* are not ordinary or average. Pay attention." He watched her chew for a moment then winked. "For two people who met, what, less than a week ago, we are remarkably honest with each other. I don't think I've ever been so honest with another person in my entire life. But it's your doing. You are open and forthright and honest and so it feels safe for me to be the same. You're refreshingly real and I'm oddly okay with it, which is weird for me. I'm a bit square you know. So, yeah, it's not ordinary."

"Mmm...interesting. But there is more really. It's not an accurate assessment of me."

"No?"

"Nope, I decided, when taking this trip I would leave the fake me behind on the island and be myself. When you hopped in the van I kept on being myself. But usually I'm quite fake, phony, superficial."

"Interesting confession. Most people who are fake, phony and, superficial are unaware they are."

"Including you? Are you fake?"

"I'd like to think I'm not but I can't go around saying what I want to all the time. Well, I can now, and I do, I guess, but I spent years behind my cop face, speaking cop words, thinking cop thoughts. And you know, I liked it. There is comfort in having a script."

"When I was young, before I was married, I had one fear."

"That was?"

"What we're talking about, being average, ordinary. I wanted to be extraordinary. To do big things. Then I chose an ordinary career, made the worst of all the ordinary mistakes including marrying the absolute worst man I could have, then chose to live a quiet life at the opposite end of the country from where I was born and basically I've spent my entire life being as boringly average as I could possibly make myself."

"And you don't think you telling me all of this without alcohol isn't extraordinary?" His smile teased but he was serious.

Charley didn't speak.

"Don't answer me if you don't want to but it is. And if I've discovered one thing on this trip so far, it's we're not average and ordinary. You might act like or think you are, I am for sure, but together *we* are not."

"Why do you think that is?"

"I don't know but I like it so far." Garry smiled and ate the last of his food. "Want to know another thing that is weird and not ordinary about us?"

"What?"

"We haven't slept together yet." He scanned her face for a reaction. She looked away, then looked back, facing his statement head on.

"Is that what ordinary, average people would be doing? After a week?" She was attracted to him. In the world of the single women she knew, attraction was followed by action.

"I'm afraid so. If they were attracted to each other like we are, sharing a room even, yeah, we would." Garry was solemn.

"Then I'm afraid, you're right. We are not average and ordinary and aren't likely to be."

"Until Quebec?" This was a hopeful question.

"At least, if at all. Garry, I'm not in that space yet. Sorry."

"And if you never are, that is fine also. I like you Charley. Either way." He raised his glass and she clinked it with hers, taking some more of the ice and chewing on it.

Would she ever be in that space? She wasn't sure but she wished she could be. If ever she wanted to be ordinary and average in any department that would be the one. But so far, she still felt dread when she thought of intimacy.

He had gone too far, too fast with her. He sensed it and wasn't surprised at her next words.

"Two rooms tonight Garry." She pushed her chair back, picking up the bill and pulling her credit card out to pay. He did the same for his bill.

Garry nodded.

Chapter 20

Moving through this country, touching upon this place and that, watching the sun rise in the morning, falling in the evening, ever at my back as I move towards the east, makes me realize Canada is an enigma. She is far too vast to feel any real intimacy with her, to get to know her to her bones. Her cities are as different as her lakes are plenty and not even halfway through the entire excursion it all feels pointless. If I can't know all of her is there any point in knowing any of her other than my own tiny habitat?

Emily Carr said, "It is wonderful to feel the grandness of Canada in the raw, not because she is Canada but because she's something sublime that you were born into, some great rugged power that you are a part of." If true, I didn't need this trip at all and could have stayed home and discovered it while I barbecued a salmon and read Leonard

Cohen's poetry. Or driven straight across and been in Newfoundland by now enjoying a cup of Tetley with Nan.

Garry knocked and she closed the journal. They hadn't shared a room for the past three nights. She opened the door to Garry holding a tray with two Tim Horton's coffees and big fat blueberry muffins.

"Are we leaving Regina? Are you ready?" Garry enjoyed the city but was ready to move on. He knew it well, having trained for the RCMP here so long ago. Some things had changed, some were the same and Charley had been kind enough to let him explore to his heart's content. She seemed to like it, in fact.

"Yep. I'm ready." She had her bag closed and was fully dressed. "Know what I was thinking?"

"Not a clue."

"I don't want to wait for Quebec." She reached up and pulled his face closed to hers and kissed him before she could think about it.

"Wait...wait." He stopped her advances.

"What? I—" She made a step backwards.

"I need to put down this coffee." He placed the tray on the table.

"Are you absolutely sure?" he inquired.

"Not even remotely. I'm just sure I want to try. You?" She met his eyes.

"Me either," he replied, honest as he pulled her close, his left hand around her back, his right her cheek. He kissed her again.

Charley wiped the tears on her cheeks with a shaking hand before she spoke, some time later.

"I'm sorry I couldn't--it wasn't better."

Garry held her close, feeling her vulnerability, not understanding but wanting to console her anyway. She was still broken. Might always be. He knew that. The most he could hope for was he wouldn't break her more. He stroked her hair, black and tangled.

"It was perfect. There is no hurry, we have an entire country to cross." He chose his words, clueless as to whether they were the right ones.

"I was raped once," she whispered. It was a lie. She had been raped multiple times.

"I thought it was something like that."

"Even after I left him, he tracked me down, took me to his place, locked me up for nearly two weeks."

"It was your husband?"

"Former husband."

"Yes."

"He was brutal, he took what he wanted when he wanted. He seemed so normal on the outside, the ultimate nice guy, do anything for anybody type but—he hated me."

"Did you report him?"

"Yes, and I left and then went back, many times. So, people stopped caring. I guess it was my fault in some ways."

"I always wondered, we took many women out of situations like that, why they went back. I have to confess I don't get it." He was earnest in wanting to understand. And because he was, she answered.

"I can't answer for everybody but for me it was because it was either a beating or death. I had no doubt leaving was a death sentence. He had told me and proved it enough. Do you know how I finally escaped? Not because I grew strong enough to leave, but because he attacked a girl, a teenager and he got arrested for that. And jailed. Not for long but enough time for me to disappear, after I was dragged through the mud by everybody for my part in it. Because they thought I knew."

"What?"

"He brought her, them it's suspected, his students, to the house. But I had no idea he was doing that to them, no idea. It was assumed I did. I didn't. I should have but I was wrapped so tightly in my own life, in my own fears, I didn't know. That's why I don't go home. People hated me for that."

"You didn't deserve any of it." He pulled her close, covering them both with the blanket.

"Didn't I?" She knew she didn't. Except in those moments when she knew she did.

"Not a bit of it. These animals are predators. You are not to blame for what happened in any way."

"I want to believe that. I've spent my entire life trying to convince myself of it. So, has my therapist. Therapists."

"Where is he now?" He hoped they wouldn't encounter the guy because in addition to being traumatic for Charley, Garry himself might have to deal him some justice.

"Dead. Dropped of a heart attack at forty-five. Sometimes life is fair." It had been the happiest day of her life and that was something she had no shame feeling.

"Good."

"It feels cowardly he had to die before I felt free again. Why can't I be braver?" She turned over, asked him face to face.

"It's not cowardly, it's self-protection."

"That's the kind of stuff my therapist says."

"Mine too." He grinned.

"I made several steps forward on this trip. I asked for help, and I've had some sort of intimacy." She smiled.

"So, you're not sorry you let me come along?" He was afraid to ask her if she was sorry about being with him physically because he didn't know if he could bear it if he had caused her more pain.

"Not yet." A genuine smile told him the answer.

"So, are we leaving Regina or not?"

"We are but I have a favour to ask you."

"Shoot." He smiled and kissed her forehead.

"Can you drive?"

"Wow. Now that's trust. I may go ten kilometers over the speed limit."

"I can handle it."

"I think you can." He kissed her on the nose.

Ten minutes later they were out of bed, their coffee nuked in the microwave and muffins devoured and when she handed him the keys he did a little dance.

"One room tonight Garry?" she asked when they were in the car, iPhone ready to book their next hotel. It wasn't perfect but his acceptance of what it was made her want more.

"Yeah, one room, one bed," he replied, "that's what I'd like if you're ok with it."

"Don't tell Nan k?" she implored him.

"Oh, my God, I forgot to tell your Nan. Hand me my phone right now, I have to call her and tell her!"

She reached across and touched his hand on the wheel and said in a gentle, quiet voice.

"Oh, fuck off."

With a big husky laugh Garry shifted the Ford into drive and screeched out of the parking spot.

Chapter 21

Charlie fidgeted. Nervous. She cleared her throat and tapped the button. She began by warning her viewers this was a serious topic she felt deserved some attention.

"I would like to spend some time tonight talking about the first people of Canada, the indigenous communities and I want to impress upon you that this is a topic I am unqualified to discuss. As much as I like to think I'm an educated, highly aware and highly engaged person, I have failed in trying to seek a better understanding of my fellow Canadians who were here first. And I freely admit it is only in the past few years I've come to understand the difficulties and troubles faced by some of their communities both in the north and here in the southern part of the country. How my ancestors signed treaties, essentially *contracts*, with them and then spent a hundred and fifty years, breaking them.

This trip is a celebration of one hundred and fifty years of this country but for those people it has been a century and a half of broken promises and broken families and the loss of country. There is no celebration for people who had their lands removed, were colonized and then, in many ways forgotten. There are people who had their children forcibly removed and sent to residential schools where a great number of them died. The rest were treated like non-humans, damaged for life, a trauma that still flows through the generations. There is no rejoicing the century and a half of loss experienced at the hands of Canada, by her first people.

These are merely words that I'm speaking. And lots of words are being spoken about reconciliation and understanding and some steps are being taken to address these issues. But there aren't enough words and the actions aren't fast enough. Children are committing suicide because of the hopelessness of their lives. *Canadian* children. And while I'm not able to visit the communities I'm talking about I've spoken to people who have. Third world conditions in Canada? This isn't the picture the international community has of us, not what's represented in tourist ads. The problems are many and I admit my guilt and past complacency. And I apologize for it.

I read the comment section of a news story last night about the Missing and Murdered Indigenous Women Inquiry and I know you're all going to say that reading the comments was a big mistake. It was not. It is important to read them because while your heart breaks that there are such ugly people with such awful hatred in their hearts, we also must know about it. You can't fix what you think doesn't exist.

Where the break in your heart occurs, is where understanding slips in. I won't waste time on those who expressed racist comments but rather say I now understand it's a big problem in this country. We can do better than this, we will not be great until all our people have access to clean water, safe and decent living conditions and hope and opportunity for a better future.

I will celebrate my country, it has been good to me. But I'll do it knowing we could have been so much better had we included our indigenous peoples for the past one hundred and fifty years. We're going to have to wear that shame and we're going to have to kick some political ass to get them to do better for the next century and a half. I'm one person but I'm one pissed-off, motivated person. I'm not going to lead this charge but I'm going to follow where the people lead me and support them to the best of my abilities. I invited you to do the same. This is Charley through Canada, signing off."

She tapped the button, flipped off her hat, slung it across the table and watched as the comments rolled up the screen. She knew there would be the usual vitriol but also there would be the positive comments, those who agreed but more importantly, those who would do better. It had been a kick in the ass to her when Garry had broken down about what he had experienced as a police officer in regions of the country where things were bad. He had traveled to communities where there was squalor and deprivation that broke his heart. She was terrified that in trying to help, it would do more harm, but still, she had to try.

Garry's key card slipped through the slider and he walked in. She looked at him and he smiled, walking to the fridge, pulling out a beer, twisting its top off and handing it to her. He did the same with a second and plopped down in a chair.

"That was good."

"It wasn't enough," Charley said. She took a swig.

"It was all you can do tonight. You don't do nothing because you can't do everything."

"Well now, aren't you the sage," she smiled, "are there foundations and places where you can help? Is there a way to do this so it doesn't look like I'm the big white hero coming to the rescue? I don't want to be that. I want to help but not in an obvious way."

"I don't know, maybe we have to ask the people who need the help. I think I'm going to do more as well. I can maybe find contacts for us. Find appropriate channels."

"Water. There are places that don't have clean water. All this makes me wonder if I should go on with this? This trip, the entire blog. I started it as a hobby you know, it's always been fun and games but it's now become something serious. It feels wrong to celebrate this country right now."

"It's perfectly fine to celebrate the good parts. But what you did there is more important."

"I guess you're right. It's good to lay out the blemishes, let the world see it all un-scrubbed and then work hard to heal them, not cover them up."

"It seems such a big job, an impossible job. But it is a job that must be done."

"I'm going to help. I don't know how but I am. I work in a school where kids are fed and clothed and happy for the most part. Yeah, there are problems but there are supports and services. I can't stand the thought of children in this country being treated so vastly different simply because they're not white."

"I know, I was shocked by it myself. But there are some success stories, some communities are overcoming it all too. Those are the examples we can use to help inspire the others who need help."

Charley drank her beer slowly, Garry was quiet beside her.

"Thank you, Garry." She tipped her bottle towards him and he clinked it with his.

"For the beer?"

"No for teaching me."

He was proving to be an asset to her on this trip and she appreciated his perspective. Sometimes an educator needed an education and Garry was providing her with that in a great many important and unexpected ways.

Chapter 22

They made their way eastward, chatting, music blasting, admiring the view. They passed by Wolseley, Grenfell, Whitewood, and finally Moosomin before crossing over into Manitoba. One short stop in Brandon for a meal, then they headed for Winnipeg.

"We have been lucky with the weather uh? This is the first time it's even been a bit cold," Charley remarked, as they entered their room at the Fort Garry Hotel. The temperature was about fifteen degrees Celsius, the lowest it had been in the city in a couple of weeks.

"Yeah. It's not always this nice in Winnipeg. Holy Jesus the winters." It had been a difficult three years, when he'd lived here.

"Ok, so we have Burton Cummings." She tried to recall what she knew about Winnipeg.

"But he lives elsewhere now?"

"And a bear named after it." Everybody knew about Winnie the Pooh.

"I thought this was weird but I remember an interview Gordon Pinsent gave and he talked about being a young teenager in Grand Falls, Newfoundland and he wanted to be an actor. So, that was unheard of, right? Well, he decided he would be one so he left, at 15 or 17, like really young and went to Winnipeg to pursue an acting career," Charley said.

"An acting career? Winnipeg? What?" Garry removed some pants and a hoodie from his bag. He shook them, trying to de-wrinkle.

"Weird, right? I have never associated Winnipeg with theater."

"Maybe Stratford, Ontario but not Winnipeg."

"Probably this was before Stratford was such a big deal. We're going there by the way."

"Will we be able to see a show? I'm not sure I'm into Shakespeare. But it's near my old hometown Tavistock, I'd like to go there."

"Sure, and as to Shakespeare, they do have other shows, musicals and so on. I get the program delivered. Subscribed when I started planning the trip so we'll try. I thought tomorrow we would go to the Canadian Human Rights Museum. Know anything about it?"

"I was so young when I lived here, I barely knew Canadian humans had rights."

"What about the ones read to them when you arrested people?" She stuck her tongue out at him, moving swiftly to avoid a butt-swat.

"Okay, the proper name is the Canadian Museum for Human Rights," she continued, reading from her iPhone.

"So, we go there tomorrow. Anywhere tonight?"

"Well, it's already late since it was after lunch before we got away."

"I was seduced, I tried to leave on time." Garry winked.

"It is my trip, I determine the schedule, don't forget that." She pointed her finger at him and he grabbed her wrist, then released it. Kissing her nose instead.

"Your wish is my command. What do you want to do?"

"Eat. Let's go down to the hotel restaurant and order something fattening."

"I need a quick shower, or are you starving?"

"Nah, go shower, I'll freshen up out here.

He grabbed a pair of pants and headed to the bathroom.

Charley pulled out her sparse cosmetic bag, raked the brush she found there through her hair and decided to leave it out of its pony tail. She rubbed some moisturizer on her face, peering at herself in the mirror. Her eyes were dark, lashes long, teeth white. Her skin was clear, though a few lines spread like rays from the corner of each of her eyes. She smiled, they weren't deep, and they vanished when she stopped smiling. Many women her age had many more laugh lines, but many women her age had laughed more.

She owned just a little make up, expensive brands and she wore it to work each day, especially lipstick. She pulled out a bright wand style gloss and applied it. She brushed a bit of blush across her cheeks and gave it all a fluff with a big brush dipped in translucent powder. She closed the make up kit and hauled on a pair of black leggings and a white tunic. She pulled a sweater out of her bag and put it on. It fell below the tunic and warmed her shoulders. She had gained a few pounds and her belly stuck out a bit. The trails of Newfoundland would make quick work of any excess pounds even if Nan cooked like calories were vitamins.

The new intimacy with Garry would improve. She could hardly scold herself for being intimate with a man after being celibate for so long. He was the nicest man she had ever met. Plus, he had Nan's endorsement. She picked up her phone.

"Charley, where are you now? Winnipeg?"
Orla Andrews answered, delight in her voice.

"You have radar Nan? Sorry I haven't called
since Regina. We stayed there for three nights
because it was so nice."

"How long are you in Winnipeg?"

"Two nights."

"You sleeping with Garry yet?"

"Nan! How did you know?" She sat on the
bed.

"Because you're a normal woman, he's a
nice-looking man, Ger told me you were sharing a
room and I figured you would be in the sack with
him soon enough. These days that's the way it
goes."

"Well, it isn't something I do at all. It's
hard."

"Well it got to be hard, wouldn't be much of
a man if it wasn't."

"Nan!" She wasn't used to her
grandmother's raunchy jokes being launched at her.

"Relax my love. You'll have a little fling
across the country. So, what of it? Be nice if you
can find a nice man, not be alone when you gets
here. Do he dance? The best men dance. Garry's a
nice bit of practice for you so you gets used to the
idea. You needs to be living, you're a beautiful
woman, still young."

"Yeah, that's it. Practice." She'd eventually be at one side of the country and he'd be at the other.

"Good for you. You can save money on rooms now. What are you doing in Winnipeg? Going to the ballet?"

"Nah, I know it's famous and all but I'm not a ballet person. We're going to Assiniboine Park, going to the Human Rights Museum, touring around tomorrow, hoping it's a bit warmer than today, first time we have had to wear pants the entire trip."

"No wonder you wound up in bed together, wearing nar pair of pants."

"Oh, my God Nan, you're awful, just awful," she said, laughing.

"What a terrible thing to say to your grandmother." Garry came up behind her.

"Hi, Mrs. Andrews," he said, pulling Charley's hand with the phone close to his mouth.

"Put me on speaker, Charlotte," her grandmother requested.

"Oh, dear Lord," Charley said, as she hit the button.

"You're sleeping with my Granddaughter now are you, young man? And I thought I could trust you. Your grandmother told me you were a gentleman but turns out you are like all the rest." Charley met Garry's eyes, noted the chagrin on his face from the scolding he was getting from Orla Andrews.

"In our family, you sleeps with a woman, you marries her, there is no fooling around with my Granddaughter, using her for your dirty pleasure and then tossing her out like garbage, capiche." She threw in the last word like she was some sort of senior citizen, outport Newfoundland mobster.

Charley's lips twitched.

Garry stammered a reply.

"We're just getting to know each other. It's too soon..." He tried, God love him.

"Wasn't too soon to defile my granddaughter." Charley made a strange hissing sound and Garry checked to see if she was okay, intense worry in his eyes. This sort of thing had to be stressful for a woman who had been through what she had been through.

"Are you okay?" He directed that to Charley then to her grandmother he said, "Mrs. Andrews, I think you should stop..." Then he noticed Charley was crying. The poor girl. No, wait, was she laughing? He heard the snort on the other end of the iPhone and it dawned on him.

"You're fucking with me aren't you Mrs. Andrews?" he asked Orla.

"You're some easy to trick b'y. You better smarten up before you gets home here. And none of this Mrs. Andrews stuff, I'm Orla."

"Orla, you got me good." He shook his head. These women were so full of pranks.

"I gets it from her," Charley spoke, her dialect breaking through her laughter.

"You two have fun. Life's too short not to have fun. Nice to know you're both having some. Gotta go put me bread on, made eight loaves of raisin, hot as Hell's flames today but don't want to be baking when you're here Charlotte." She'd dropped the aitches from *hell's* and *here* but had added a couple to *Orla* and *Andrews*.

"Thanks Nan, I love you."

"I love you too sweetheart."

"I hate you both." Garry said, his broad grin belying his words.

"Oh my, the look on your face," Charley laughed, shaking her head, "c'mon, let's go eat."

Chapter 23

Assiniboine Park with nearly 1200 acres of lush green foliage enthralled and bewitched its visitors. After a morning of exhaustive exploration Charley and Garry worked up an appetite just walking around, checking out the place and talking. Starved, they settled in at The Park Cafe.

"I love this place. I think this is my favourite city so far," Charley said, the magic of the place had her longing to spend more time. She wasn't the only one. There were streams of people milling about, many headed to, or coming from, the zoo.

She was halfway through her Chicken Apple Chutney sandwich, with its delicious arugula, tomato and curried mayo, while Garry was enjoying a chicken Pesto wrap. It was still cooler than the rest of the country but had hit twenty degrees so they had tied their sweaters around their waists.

"This park certainly is wonderful." Garry agreed recalling their morning spent strolling the gardens, exploring the art displayed in The Pavilion, meandering around the Leo Mol Sculpture Garden, with its statues of ladies bathing or lounging in a fountain, along with other bronze works set among lush flowers and foliage.

"Can we stay in Winnipeg for a month?" Charley was smitten by the tiny bit of the city she had seen.

"You like it that much?"

"I love it. There is so much here in this one spot that speaks to me. Every bit of this place, even the crowds, are calming. There is a good energy."

Garry raised an eyebrow.

"Some places feel good; do you know what I mean?"

"Yeah, Yellowknife. I went there to visit a cop friend a couple of years ago. I could live there, I loved the feel of the place. I absolutely get what you mean?"

"Bowen Island feels that kind of good. It's become home but if I ever decide I want to live elsewhere and Winnipeg is an option, I'd be excited."

"And you get all that from one morning?"

"How long did it take you to get it in Yellowknife?"

"Probably a day and a half."

She laughed. "Why didn't you stay then? That would have been after you were injured, right? You could live anywhere."

"It was right after that. But I had medical things in Vancouver."

"Rehab?"

"Something like that."

"Therapy?"

"A lot of that. Yellowknife would have been a diversion."

"And you can go back. I mean, after you have spent time with your grandmother, if it turns out it doesn't suit, you can go there?"

"I suppose I can, but Nan would be pretty upset if I left her again too soon."

"Excuse me but can I share this table? The place is full." A man and a child of about five were standing, holding food.

"Oh, yes, please, we're nearly done." Their table for four was the only one in the area with any free chairs.

"I'm Brad, this is Eric." He motioned to the child to say hello.

"Hi, I'm Eric," the boy repeated, then lowered his head when the adults laughed.

"I apologize Eric," Charley spoke, "it's rude to laugh at people. We found your cuteness unexpected. We are Charley and Garry."

"Ok. Do you have a little boy?" The child held up a small toy giraffe, presumably purchased at the zoo gift shop.

"I don't, but I teach little kids who are five and six years old. You have been to the zoo I see, we're going next. Was it enjoyable?" she spoke, addressing him like a peer, not like a child. She wasn't the cutesy-wutesy type.

"Yep, want a bubble gum?" He held out two pieces to Garry and Charley, and after they thanked him, picked up a fork and started to eat his macaroni and cheese.

"Where are you guys from?" Brad asked, his dark eyes friendly and curious.

"I'm from Bowen Island in British Columbia and Garry is from Vancouver but moving to Newfoundland. We're traveling across the country, seeing some sights."

"What a great thing to do. I'm from here, brought Eric here for the day, I get him for summers, his mom lives in Ottawa."

"Well it's a great city, Winnipeg. I was just saying how much I love it."

"It is, there are problems but there are many nice things. You hear the bad stuff on the news."

"Yeah, my impression is completely changed in a morning." Charley enthused.

"Have you been to the Human Rights Museum?"

"Next stop for us." Garry wiped his fingers on his napkin, his wrap gone.

"It's pretty powerful stuff. I won't take Eric, lot to explain to a kid. A lot to explain to me. Holocaust stuff. Makes you wonder."

"Wonder what?" Charlie asked.

"If we are any better here. Could it happen to us? What would I do if it did? Would I be brave and help? Run and get out? Join in? I have a child, so would I go along to protect him? You know, lighthearted things like that. Sorry, that's too heavy for lunch with strangers."

"No, no, not at all. In fact, we've been pondering things like across the country. Heavy questions." She nodded in understanding.

"Well, if people are pondering, there is a chance for us. It's when we stop pondering we're in big trouble." Brad smiled, glancing at his son who was engaged, playing with his toy.

"I agree. We'll keep your questions in mind while we tour. I'm glad you joined us Brad." She was finished eating and she stood up, Garry copied her.

"Eric, you have fun," Garry said.

"Thanks for letting us sit here." The two of them went back to their food as Garry and Charley walked away.

"Let's do the zoo first. And that's not because I think it's more important, but because I think I need to have time after the museum to process it." Charley said.

"I think that's a good idea."

Garry reached out and took her hand, the first time he had done so, holding it as they walked. Charley was uncomfortable at first, this kind of intimacy as foreign to her as the pleasure they now shared with each other in bed.

But she held it . This trip was about doing new things, learning about her country and as she was finding out, about herself. And now, learning about Garry too.

She didn't know what his whole story was yet though he had alluded to a therapist several times. Dealing with an injury that cost him his career might be all there was but didn't explain the mystery of why he wouldn't fly home. Nan told her he had gotten a nice inheritance from his parents' estate. He wasn't budgeting this trip at all so money wasn't the issue.

All thoughts of Garry's secrets vanished when they began their trek through the eighty acres or so that made up the zoo. Over two hundred species of animals called it home and Garry was as likely to "awww-luh" over the polar bears as Charley who became enamored of Nanuq and Siku,

Inuit names meaning polar bear and ice, respectively. All the exhibits were fun and educational but this one turned them both into puddles with its sweetness.

"I want a polar bear," Charley lamented.

"I don't think that's advisable," Garry said.

"Just a little one…they are sooo cute." She could have been the same age as the kid, Eric, who had share their lunch table as she closed her eyes and stomped her feet, demanding just a little one.

"Come on kid, let's take the tram back, we still have the human rights museum to go to."

"I never get anything I want," she pouted, then winked at him.

"You get everything you want, and you know it." He still held her hand and helped her into the little vehicle with a dozen or so people already on board.

"I do." She sat next to him, her hand folded into his, the trolley moving along, showing some of the things they had already seen, having already walked most of the large zoo.

"Do you know what?" Garry asked. He had enjoyed this day so much, the entire trip so far .

"What?"

He leaned in close, whispering into her ear.

"I like you. I mean I *like* like you."

Charley smiled at him, a glint in her eye, and said loud enough for the entire trolley to hear.

"I like-like you too Garry," with a huge emphasis on the first like.

Garry erupted with laughter and everybody looked at the couple, some baffled, others, who overheard the entire exchange, laughed along.

"I should have known," he said, shaking his head.

"Yeah," Charley agreed, with an exaggerated wink, blowing a huge bubble with the gum Eric had given her and popping it with a big splat, "ya should have."

Chapter 24

In Canada, privilege is rampant. For most it means having problems in your life, overcoming them, recovering, rebuilding and moving forward without the added hardship of being born in brown skin, or Jewish skin, or Muslim skin or even female skin. Even I, a white woman, have privilege, over a woman in any of the other colour. I wonder what it's like to be a white man with all the glory that entails, with your needs superior, your thoughts parsed and praised simply because they're yours.

Privilege is the reason my abuse wasn't prevented, why I wasn't safe to exit that horror. It is because of it I was expected to behave a certain way. Still am, though I'm stronger now. But is that only because I'm traveling in the shadow of this new white man? His apparent approval of me, bolsters my approval of myself. I wonder why I couldn't lift myself up? Why I needed him.

Charley shot a glance over to where Garry slept, his head denting the deep pillows of the hotel room, his soft breathing like that of a child. She felt a twinge of guilt for her words, true as they were. He might have his troubles but his advantages were also there. If they had a chance of having even a friendship beyond this fling, then she would have to know he understood he had this privilege. She would settle for nothing less than someone who understood that. She continued her writing, her journal part of her recovery from her past and a regular habit in her life.

Or maybe it's his kindness that has given me strength? Maybe I should take more credit for my own part in my recovery. Perhaps I didn't need him, but rather he was just a catalyst in my fixing myself. As I suspected, in the center of this country that I set out to explore, I am learning as much about myself as I am about it, perhaps more.

She jotted the date above the journal entry and tossed the book in her bag. Garry turned over, his face straight up at the ceiling, his hands clenched in fists at his side and Charley gasped. Was he having a seizure?

She flew to the bed and reached out trying to recall her first aid training.

She touched his arm.

"Garry," she shook him a bit, "are you okay?"

His fist struck out. It sent her backwards across the bed. Garry screamed and sat upright. Charley jumped up and fled to the door, a hand on her burning cheek.

The terror of years-ago swept through her and she felt a rush of fear in her veins. Not again, not another man being violent towards her. Her instincts said run but then she heard a fear and torment in his voice as great as her own.

"Not now, not now, no," Garry said, the words senseless. Charley moved back, watching him. He was asleep still, though he sat.

She walked across the room to put some distance between them. She was scared for herself but also for him. She opened the hotel room door, prepared to run, not quite knowing what she was dealing with, her face sore from the blow she now understood to be accidental.

"Garry, wake up," she ordered. Garry's eyes flew open, he looked across the room at her and then at the bed.

"What?" Why did you wake me? Is something wrong?"

"You were, I mean, I thought you were having a seizure but perhaps a nightmare?" She was relieved he was awake and seemed to be fine.

"Fuck, I haven't had one in a long time. What did I say?"

"You didn't say anything that made sense, I touched you to wake you and you, well, you hit me in the face. And you screamed."

"What? I hit you, oh my God. I am so sorry." He swung his legs over the side of the bed, put his head in his hands.

"It's alright, you were asleep." She was less shaken now.

"I should sleep in a separate room. I haven't slept with anybody in so long, I didn't know that could happen, I don't even know what to say to you right now."

"There isn't anything to say, I could have done the same thing in the throes of a nightmare, come on."

"That's where I hit you?" He grabbed his glasses off the nightstand and peered at her red cheek.

"It's not bad, it was mostly, a fright."

"No, it was not just a fright, it is awful. I don't know what to say to you. This isn't good, I need to make a call."

"Okay, I'll go downstairs, get a coffee, eat breakfast, book tomorrow's hotel, text me when you're ready to join me." She grabbed her phone and her journal, and left him sitting on the bed, his face taut and serious.

Charley sat in the Broadway Breakfast Room. She smiled as the waitress who had served them the day before came by to take her order.

"Boyfriend sleeping in?" she asked. They were super friendly here.

"He's running a bit late and needed to make some calls." She ordered a hot breakfast, her appetite big despite the drama of ten minutes earlier.

She flipped open her journal.

Sitting in the Fort Garry Hotel, we're not even two weeks into this trip and after all of my deliberations on privilege I find myself smacked in the face by reality, literally. Garry appears to have some sort of mental health issue. I don't know what but he acted violent in his sleep this morning though it was defensive I think. When I touched him, he struck back. I know this happened while he was asleep, and I know it is useless to ask Nan what she thinks. When he was injured, perhaps it led to some sort of post-traumatic disorder, like you hear about all over the news. He has a therapist, he has been wounded in the line of duty, and there is something wrong. He is on the phone with somebody now, his grandmother perhaps. I guess I'll have to wait for answers but I must admit, I'm impressed by how little I am traumatized by being hit by a man. It didn't send me back there, didn't make me feel weak, except for a moment and in fact, I was clear-headed enough to make myself safe, then deal with it. How I'll feel tonight when we go to bed together,

I'm not sure. But we will go to bed together and that decision right there, she saw him coming out of her peripheral vision, *is why I'm feeling particularly brave,* she finished.

"Coffee, and whatever she's having," he directed the waitress who saw him sit down.

"You're okay?" Charley asked him.

"Embarrassed, apologetic, but yeah, I'm fine. It was a dream. I've never struck a woman before, you understand, that, right? How are you?" He stared at her red cheek.

"Yes, I do understand and I'm fine. Look, Garry, are you ever going to tell me? Maybe you should."

"Yeah, but can I tell you another time? But before we get home? Maybe on the ferry?"

"Okay, that's a deal Tell you what, let's head to Ontario uh?"

"Are you driving?"

"Yeah, I want to stop in Northern Ontario, then on to Stratford. We'll spend some time there."

"Did you book our rooms?"

"Room. Yes. We are going to keep sharing. Let's put this behind us for now. Look I had a thought. I know you're a fan of the Leafs and I'm a Canadiens fan but it's about eight hours to Thunder Bay, then another ten to eleven hours to Parry Sound, and well there is something in Parry Sound I want to see."

"The Bobby Orr Museum, right?" He looked thrilled.

"That's good for you? It's a Hall of Fame. And although I am a Habs fan I never could get on board with the whole Bruins rivalry because my Dad was a huge Bruins/Bobby Orr fan. I booked a room an hour past Thunder Bay, then another in Parry Sound. Ontario is some vicious size, as Nan would say."

"Ontario is like its own planet." He made a big circular shape with his hands to accentuate his point. He was relieved at the ease with which she moved on from the morning's drama. God, he was embarrassed.

"Then we leave Parry Sound, go to Stratford, where we'll spend a few days, do laundry, before heading to Quebec, which is up to you to plan because you know, we're having a date there."

"You're sure you're okay?" He could still see a shade of the blow he had dealt her. His therapist said it was something people did sometimes and he needed to not stress about it. He had also said he was pleased he had met somebody but to be careful about attachments when they were going to end up on opposite ends of the country after this trip. It had set Garry back a little to hear out loud that after she visited her grandmother, she would be going to Bowen Island alone. And he certainly couldn't go back with her, that would be creepy.

"Earth to Garry," Charley snapped her fingers.

"I'm here and so is breakfast."

Charley watched him a moment before picking up her fork.

"Ok, then Bobby Orr Museum it is."

"Yes!" A bit of the old Garry's enthusiasm broke through.

Charley dug in, voracious now things were settled with Garry. She hoped he held to his promise to tell her what was up with him soon, she didn't want any other surprises. As much as she liked him, a repeat would have him at a bus station before he could say sorry. She had safeguarded herself from violence for a long time, and she wouldn't allow it in her life again no matter what sort of demons caused Garry to lash out. His issues were his, she had her own troubles to deal with.

Plus she was damned curious. What the hell was his problem?

Chapter 25

Garry and Charley made their way across northern Ontario, through the landscape of the Canadian shield. It was over three and a half billion years old, Garry read out loud from his iPhone near Thunder Bay when they once more accessed the Internet. There was a complete lack of cell phone service over much of the vast and sparsely-populated area. Lakes, bogs, trees and rocks comprised the scenery of the route as they traveled further and further eastward.

It was during this bit of research by Garry that they learned about Sleeping Giant Provincial Park and decided to delay everything by one day to hike the trails.

They glared at a distant land formation. Frustrated.

"I still don't make out any sort of sleeping giant, do you?" Charley squinted her eyes, looking across at the long peninsula.

"I thought it would be more obvious." Garry stared also, from the spot where they'd been advised by a local they would be able to see it, lulling on its back, in profile.

"I can't see it through the zoom either." Charley peered through her camera. Garry's occasional driving enabled her to photograph and update her social media with new photos every day. Her followers, impressed, encouraged her to post more.

"What if we rent a canoe instead of hiking? Do you canoe?"

"I do and I love it, it's been a long time since I've been in one. I kayak too."

"I've never been in a kayak and I think I'd rather stick with what I know right now. I hope to go kayaking when we get home, though Nan's boat is pretty great too."

"I'd love to do that with you." Garry smiled at her. It was nice having a companion. He saw the attraction in a long-term relationship now, having eschewed such commitments his whole life.

It took a short time to find a place to rent a canoe and soon they were on the water, the supposed sleeping giant now a view of several broad chunks of land that from another vantage point claimed to show the lazing leviathan.

They paddled along, the lake still, the morning bright and warm. There wasn't another boat in sight, not another human as they made their way outward then turned so they remained parallel to the shore, moving as one, their strokes hitting the water in tandem, breaking the surface with precision, then rising, forward and cutting again. The rote motion loosened up Charley's shoulders, stiffened from hours of her hands on the wheel. She heard Garry behind her, his breath even, his paddling strong, their motion through the water smooth and unencumbered.

"I don't know if I should speak. This is so incredible," he said, tone reverend.

"I read somewhere that experiencing a feeling of awe regularly increases a person's overall happiness level," Charley responded.

"Well there is an abundance of awe here, it has all the awe."

"Yep, every bit of the awe. It's gorgeous. I can't believe there's nobody but us out here on the lake."

"It's early and a weekday," he said, recalling the glorious sunrise as they headed to the park.

"So, it's all ours for a while." Charley sliced the water, loving the feeling of sitting on its surface, the pull of the canoe as it slid forward, the gentle rush of the wake behind them.

They moved along until Charley spotted a land formation and suggested they pull in, take some pictures, have a snack.

The canoe turned with their paddle strokes towards a structure that looked like a loop, the rocks going around overhead. It was named the Sea Lion per the information pamphlet at Silver Islet.

Click-click-click went the Canon as Charley photographed it from every angle, getting as close as possible to the strange arch.

"This thing is fascinating and it has some sort of bright yellow moss on it." She switched to a Macro lens to get some close up shots.

"It's called Sunburst Lichen if I recall and I can see why."

"Yeah, it looks sun-shiny." The canoe tipped a bit as she pivoted to put the camera back in its case, then flipped her feet around to face Garry. "This is nice. We should do more of this nature stuff."

"Whatever you want to do is fine by me. I did a lot of this kind of thing in the north. It puts you in touch with the land, makes you wonder about the history, who went before."

"Thanks Mr. Accommodating. Did you know there is a legend about the Sleeping Giant? I read he's an Ojibwa Warrior who displeased the Gods when he tried to stop people from getting to the silver vein on the other side of the mountain. It's the largest silver vein around you know, so anyway, the Great Spirit was angry with him and turned him to stone, his name was-I memorized it-Nanabijou, something like that, and he laid down at the end of the peninsula, to protect Silver Islet."

"That is a great story. So many stories live here in this land. I always think, what are we but our stories. We all have tales to tell, many of them."

"What's your story Han Solo?"

"Well after I stopped smuggling goods to the Jabba and went on to save the universe, I became a police officer, a job I failed at spectacularly."

"You think you failed at it? Why? Because you were injured?"

"Many reasons, I'm hoping to succeed at the rest of my life however. This trip is fairly successful. What's your story?"

"I am a school teacher who failed spectacularly at marriage by marrying a sociopath, but who has done well creating a quiet and frugal life, allowing me to pay off a house on Bowen Island, which now leaves me enough disposable income to travel a bit. So, semi-successful but rather boring."

"Boring is underrated." Garry offered her a bottle of water.

"But it's still boring. This trip isn't though. It's fun."

"I'm glad you're enjoying it. I'm not interfering too much?"

"You've already interfered a great deal, not in a bad way but—" The word hung there, suspended between them.

"What?"

"Well, we are getting close, aren't we? I mean, we get along well, we have developed a physical relationship, we have a ton in common, we like each other, we are acting like a couple. Have you given any thought to after?"

"After what? After we get home to Newfoundland?"

"Newfoundland isn't home for me. British Columbia is. So, after I return to British Columbia and you're in Newfoundland this is over right? You don't have expectations beyond that?"

"To be honest, I hadn't given it much thought." He had shuffled it to the back of his mind. He didn't like how it felt when he thought about it, so he didn't.

"That's OK, I mean, this is nice. I am enjoying every moment of this trip. You're a nice guy Garry but I'm staying home for a while then turning around with Nan and driving back. That's it for you and me. After I leave."

"Yeah."

Charley noted a familiar sadness in her heart, a grief for what couldn't be, a gripping feeling of despair for a lost possibility, and she twisted her legs back over the seat of the canoe. She faced forward and straightened her back. Foolish. She needed to learn to be disappointed, to enjoy the moment and not think about what could or couldn't happen. Like Garry. He was quite unperturbed by the idea of the eventual end to their friendship.

Garry followed her lead, dipping his paddle into the serene lake, raising it into the warm air, dropping it back down again, enthralled by the unparalleled beauty. But sadness gripped his heart. He like-liked her and perhaps they could have been more, been permanent over time. This trip through Canada wasn't long enough. The country was big enough to fall in love driving through, but far *too* big to maintain that love if they lived on opposite coasts. So, he simply wouldn't fall in love with her. That should be easy. Love hadn't been a place he'd ever fallen into in his entire life. Why start now?

His paddle struck the water a millisecond behind hers and he tried to get back into the rhythm but it took awhile to synchronize their strokes again. Charley noticed but didn't mention it. Eventually their rhythm matched once more, the tiny vessel propelling them forward on Lake Superior, where a sleeping giant protected the silver, and sunburst lichens wrapped the rocks in gold.

Even melancholy thoughts couldn't tarnish the day and by the time they reached the shore all of them had vanished into the warm air. When they boarded her car again, they were each settled in their minds. They would enjoy the trip then move on from each other in a healthy way when the time came. There was no other way.

Chapter 26

It was too late to go to the museum when they arrived in Parry Sound so they checked into the Comfort Inn, its basic accommodations included breakfast which was great for a quick overnight stop. Charley offered Garry the van to go exploring, telling him she needed a bit of alone time in the hotel. Things had been a tad awkward between them after their serious conversation at the lake. The drive had been quiet, their thoughts in other places.

With a few hours of daylight remaining he set off to check out a few of the small towns. He thought he'd go to Britt, located near one of the inlets leading out to Georgian Bay from the Magnetewan River that poured into Lake Huron.

Charley picked up a bottle of wine and some KFC and snacks before he left. She devoured the chicken and was deep into a bag of Miss Vicki's Potato chips.

She wandered around the small room, a wine glass cupped between two fingers in her left hand.

"Come on, Charlotte, *Charley*," she spoke aloud, "it's a phone call. You've managed to travel across the country with a strange man, you've broken through your fear of intimacy, you've not panicked when a man punched you in the face when you used to be triggered by television shows showing a woman getting smacked. Surely you can make one tiny call." She downed the wine.

"And you can do it sober." She stopped in front of a wall mirror. "And you can do it sober," she repeated.

She picked up her phone, pulled up the number from her contacts and hit it, her face scrunched up as though an explosion were pending. Julia answered right away.

"It's Charley, er, Charlotte. Um, Andrews. I thought I'd call, say hi." She was only known as Charlotte at the school.

"Oh, my God, how is the trip? Is everything alright? You sound funny." The voice at the other end was friendly, happy to hear from her.

"It's great. Really good. We're in Parry Sound, arrived here a short while ago." Charlotte let out a breath, releasing some of the tension.

"We? I thought you were alone." Julia jumped on that tidbit.

"I was supposed to be. It's a long story. All good at the house?" Julia Price taught at the school with Charlotte, starting there a year before her. She also lived two houses from her, was single and it was Julia who alerted Charley to the private sale that got her a great price on her home fifteen years earlier. But they never became true friends. She thought early on Julia was trying to forge a closeness but Charley resisted and instead a friendly acquaintanceship formed rather than an intimate friendship.

"I figured as much. Just here alone in the hotel, thought I'd call for a bit of a chat, unless it's a bad time."

"No, it's fine, it's fine. Look, I'm outside on the deck, let me go in, grab a glass of wine, we'll have a good gab."

"Sounds great." A gab. When was her last gab with a friend? Her final year at university?

"The weather has been fantastic out here these past weeks, hardly any rain, how has it been on your trip?" Julia settled into her chaise lounge and picked up the sunscreen, tossing a glob into her hand and applying it to her legs.

"It's been over twenty except for a couple of days, Winnipeg was in the mid-teens. No rain worth mentioning." Nearly every conversation in the country started with the weather.

"So, who is the man?"

"How did you know there's a man?" Charley nearly choked on her wine.

"You never call me for a chat, you have somebody on the trip with you, now you call. That's often what women chat about you know? Men."

"Well guess that's why I never call to chat. No men." She laughed, caught. There were many things Charley would like to talk about other than men, but this time, Julia had guessed right.

"Oh, don't get me wrong, don't get me wrong at all, women chat about serious non-man related stuff all the time, as you know, but a special, unexpected call, well, it was an educated guess—so where is he now? Who is he ?"

Charley went into a narrative on her Nan's part in the whole thing, then forayed into their getting together as a couple.

"It sounds like you have a good chemistry with this guy, wicked. It's about time I say, nice to have a man in your life. I'd be in a very bad mood if I went so long as you did. We thought you might like women but with a few eligible ladies around and you not showing interest in them either it was a bit confusing."

"Eligible ladies? I didn't even know. Like you?" she inquired.

"Nope, I like the boys but there are some around. Why the swearing off men? One of them did stuff?"

"My ex-husband, abusive ex-husband. Long story."

"Well at least it wasn't your father…" Julia's voice was quiet.

"God, no, he was a saint. Wait, you?" It took a moment to realize what Julia meant.

"Yeah, stepfather actually, nasty asshole, I was sixteen, mom believed me and tossed him out but it did some damage. I don't tell everyone, but you aren't the gossipy type," she said to Charlotte.

Julia wasn't either, in the staffroom she avoided conversations about others, and never seemed to have a negative word to say. Charley was the same. Had she taken some interest in real relationships with people, she wouldn't have shared any of Julia's secrets.

"But you have no problems dating, you're always off on escapades. You're always talking about finding a man and settling down." Julia was known to date a lot and share her experiences, usually in a light-hearted way.

"I am, and I will. I'm determined I won't die alone, but I'm also picky so, it may take time. Meanwhile I'm having fun, but this Garry thing—it's serious?"

"Nope, well, it might have had potential but he's moving to the far east and I'm going to visit Nan to end off my big Canada tour. I'll be back on the left coast in a few weeks, so nope, not going to be more than what it is now. Which is fine."

"Except you wish it could be more." Julia was spot on.

"Perhaps, but I shouldn't settle for the first man I like after years of avoiding men ."

"Or you should grab on to the first man you like, if you like him enough and he's worth it. Good men are scarce, trust me, I know." She rolled her eyes as though Charley could see her face.

"It's not like the romance books, there is not a great romance thing, he's a bit of a nerd, at least for a Mountie, a reader, a thinker, a conservative of all things, but with an open mind, he listens well, and he's very patient. Yeah, I like him."

"Did he vote for Stephen Harper?" Julia was horrified. She was a card-carrying member of The Green Party.

"Yeah, isn't that crazy?"

"Run, run like the wind, save yourself," Julia joked.

"I know, right? But he's not what you think. We're far more alike than we're different."

"Aww, he sounds like a nice guy. You should see if he'll move out to the island, you have a big house for one person."

"I'm not going to invite a man I have known for a couple of weeks to live with me." The idea was preposterous.

"Invite him to fly out, stay for a month. See how it goes." Julia would do that.

"He doesn't fly." But why? If he was afraid to fly, then own up to it. Lots of people were but somehow, the lengths to which their grandmothers went through to not tell her why was making her think it was much more.

"That's a weird thing. Why doesn't he fly? Chicken? It's true, chickens can't fly," She giggled at her lame joke. "I'd have to find out why, if it were me."

"Yeah, I have to too. I have a question for you."

"Ask away." Julia stretched out on the lounge admiring her tanned legs, waiting.

"You're always so confident, you date, you have a lot of friends, you always talk about finding Mr. Right, yet you always seem so happy to be single too. What's the trick?"

"Well, I am, I'm happy. But I wasn't always and in fact it's only been recently I've settled into being content. Do you know I turned down a date last week, because I had plans with some friends? I used to always accept dates, making my life around them, trying to find a man. But one morning not that long ago, I woke up, looked over at the empty space beside me and thought something that changed my life forever."

"What was that?" Charley leaned forward, on her bed, listening, her phone plugged in to get a charge so she had put the call on speaker.

"I decided to be grateful for what I had, to appreciate the life I live and not to waste my time on people who weren't worth the effort. And you know what else I'm grateful for?"

"What?" Charley chewed a chip, stopping so she could hear the answer without it being muffled by the crunch.

"I thank the Lord above, Mother Nature and the Gods of Ancient Greece and Rome every single day that I'm not Melania-goddamn-Trump."

Charley's explosive laugh sent Miss Vicki's chewed chip crumbs across the bed.

"I know, right? Oh, my God, imagine having that ugly, fat, old orange thing crawling on you? Alone is better." She brushed some chip crumbs off her pillow.

"I'm pretty grateful for the fact I'm not married to that pussy-grabbing pervert. There isn't enough money on planet earth. Gross uh?" Julia grinned, turned over to tan her back. It would be nice to have a man around to apply sunscreen though, she thought.

"I'd die of plague and smallpox in a most painful fashion before I'd have that thing in my bed." Charley agreed, and they both broke into new gales of laughter.

Chapter 27

Charley sized up her leg. There were varying degrees of tan, dark between her socks and halfway up her calf, less dark from her calf to her mid-thigh and then white above that. She pulled her night shirt down, still listening to Julia's wisdom on men.

"The real winner was this guy I was seeing who was married. I know, judge away, you would be right. So, of course he was *soooo* in love with me. And unlike in most of these cases he left his wife, wanted to move out here with me from Vancouver, wanted us to be together because, you see, I *saved* him, he would say. It was a strange relationship. We were constantly in touch by text, he became my emotional crutch in a lot of ways, my way of feeling needed I guess. I'd been on my own, was so lonely, for so long. Then, one day he started to slip away, it changed, he stopped replying right away and I was so confused, we had been so close. He adored me. I was his soul mate and all that bullshit I was so eager to believe."

"What happened? He went back to his wife?"

"No, he blamed it all on stress from his situation with custody and the ex-wife and so on, so I dumped him. Figured I must be adding to the stress. It was difficult. I left a voice mail releasing him and as much as I was sad to lose him, I was relieved too. He was so friggin' needy and I knew it was the right thing. There was something *off*. Instinct is important in dealing with people. But I made the mistake of offering to be friends. Never offer to be friends after a break up."

"That wasn't a good thing?" She hoped her and Garry would be friends after.

"No, never. Anyway, the minute I ditched him, suddenly it seemed like he was back, though not quite the same as before. Then he confided he was sick, he was trying to put on a brave front for his family, hadn't told them he was facing such illness but had cancer and was taking radiation. Well, as a friend I couldn't abandon him, right?"

"Of course not."

"And so, we started to get close again. It was mostly skyping and texting. I was here, he was in Vancouver and we couldn't see each other much, it was right towards the end of the school year. Plus, he needed to spend time with his kids and his ex-wife wouldn't allow him to have them if she caught a whiff of me being in the picture. You see, she knew about me and hated me."

"As you would expect." Charley *had* judged a bit.

"Yep, don't blame the woman at all."

"So then, I decide, I can't do this, I don't love the man, it's getting to be too much, and so I end it again. This time I lie and tell him I'm in love with somebody else because it seemed like the best way to have it end for good. And he appears to handle it quite well. I felt so guilty though, he had cancer..."

"That's good. But yeah, that was hard I bet." Charley nibbled at a Lindt chocolate bar and sipped her red wine, fascinated.

"Yeah, except that same night his Facebook relationship status changes to *in a relationship* with another woman. And it's this woman he had told me was pursuing him but that she was crazy, and he had blocked her on Facebook, the whole nine yards. But you know what? I had suspected as much, the sudden distance, he had found another, more convenient person, her name had come up a few times and I encouraged him to see her when it did but he always said, oh no, I was the love of his life, blech. I was a bit pissed but I still worried about him and we had agreed to keep in occasional contact. I never let on I noticed his Facebook status change. Then, about a month after that I get a text at around 11:30pm at night. Guy needs to talk to me. So, I call him, after all, we're not enemies. And I kind of missed him too you know. So he tells me he's been told he only has six months to live."

Julia paused so Charlotte could let this sink in.

"Oh, my God, that's awful." A tear fell down Charley's cheek. No wonder the guy was all over the place. And poor Julia, to lose a friend like that.

"Yeah, he hasn't told anyone, he says, and he's going to visit his kids, he needs support, he needs to see me sometime. He has nobody to tell, the new girlfriend isn't in the picture anymore, she was a friend, she was a rebound but it couldn't go anywhere. I was the love of his life, and, after all, he has nothing to offer her or me or anyone. It was heartbreaking. I was a mess. His two little children. My heart was torn for them all. I considered taking a leave from school to go be with him for six months. I didn't though. So anyway, I reassured him I'd be there for him. That I would do what I could to support him because that's what you do right?"

"I'm so sorry, that must have been awful." She wiped the tear away, sad for the guy who most likely was gone by now. Julia continued the story.

"It was torture, I kept in touch with him. I kept thinking of his poor little kids with no Dad. I did the math, counting ahead the six months after which he would most likely be gone. He would text me before radiation, tell me about his MRI's and radiation treatments. It was so painful, to hear him speak of that, going into the treatment, then twenty minutes to an hour later a text saying he was out. I reassured him, and set aside everything so I could be there for him, made him a priority."

"This is the saddest story ever." Charley was immersed in the tragedy, her heart breaking for the young man, his children, her friend.

"Yeah, you have no idea. It tore me apart. So anyway, let me finish. Where was I?"

"He texted you before radiation, you were there for him." Charley said.

"Right, so then he's getting less into communication, after a few weeks, then for some reason he blocks me on Facebook, but he tells me he took it down, he didn't want it to be up after he died. Which makes sense. Then though, the shocker. I hear through the grapevine he has moved in with his girlfriend, this is a few months after he has told me he's dying."

"What?" Charley sat up. She hadn't expected this twist.

"It's crazy, so he's dying right, at this point he has maybe three or four months to live and he's starting a domestic relationship. I'm a bit pissed. He misled me, yes, but this is good. I'm free. He is *her* concern now. Obviously, she knows and she is going to be his support and as awful as this situation is, I am relieved of the burden of being available for his every need, even if it is long distance. Talk about emotional labour, right? Hang on, gonna get a refill of wine." She took the phone with her, putting it on the bar.

"I understand, you would do that for a stranger so for sure you would do it for a friend. So, what happened? How long did he live?" Charley was invested in this story now. She opened a second bag of Miss Vicki's, drained the bottle of wine into her glass and waited.

"He lasted for, let me see, that was in two thousand and two, it's now two thousand and seventeen and he's going strong."

"What the fuck?" Charley was incredulous. "Was it some sort of medical miracle? What the actual fuck?"

"What the actual fuck is exactly it," Julia laughed, "it took me a year to accept it but he was never dying." She spat the word *never*.

"No! What? He lied about being terminally ill with cancer? Who the fuck does that?" This was the worst sort of emotional abuse.

"Well my best guess, according to my research, because that fucked me up, you know, so I have researched the hell out of it, is he's either a covert narcissist or a manipulating liar but I'm going with the former because if you saw his Facebook, it was always full of these amazing things. He marched in Gay pride parades, though he wasn't gay, he helped people get tickets for shows, treated people to all these expensive things, he donated blood, he donated money, all of which would get him tons of kudos but in real life he was a bastard to those closest to him. I feel sorry for the woman he wound up with."

"They got married?"

"I have no idea but last I heard they were engaged. I moved on, I sort of slipped out of his life, and never contacted him again. I have always felt a sordid curiosity about whether he repeated the pattern, she would be his third wife, and both the others were raving lunatics according to him but I think now, he was an emotional abuser, who drove them crazy. And I had a lucky escape. And he never drove me crazy. I never once lost my temper or railed on him for his awfulness because at no point would I allow him to control my emotions after the initial shutting me out. I think that's partly why he told me he was dying, figured I'd finally lose it on him, when he actually lived. It became a challenge. I won it."

"Wow, so you never confronted him? I think I would have flipped out on him. That is a wild story. I can't believe someone would do such a thing."

"Here is the other thing, that makes it worse. Both his father and his brother died of cancer. To use that disease to try to manipulate me back in his life, there is a serious flaw there."

"He's mentally ill. Or something." Charley was still reeling from the story.

"Personality disorder or an asshole, and not mentally ill. Mentally ill people are sick. He knew what he was doing. He wasn't sick, he was evil."

"Yeah you're right. I should learn more about mental illness."

"Because of Garry?" Her story done, Julia brought the topic back around to Charley's situation.

"Something's up there, I suspect so. He takes a medication. I Googled and it treats depression."

"Mmm, yeah, well then he's had depression. Has it. I'm not sure there is a cure, though I've been years now without a relapse. I suffered with it in my twenties so if that is it you can always call me to get some insight into what it's about, if you need to."

Charley told her about the dream, and the punch and Julia agreed, he couldn't be held accountable for his actions while sleeping.

"I think that's an entirely different issue. He sounds safe, I would go very, very, slowly with him, with anyone. You could end up with a creep like the living-dead guy…that's what I call him. I don't like to say his name out loud, my blood pressure goes up."

"Well the living-dead guy is a complete asshole, and I'm with you, his poor wife. Wives. Kids. He's a real piece of work."

"I'm not trying to scare you off men, there are nice ones out there, like the guy I brushed off a while ago. I am drawn to him. But on my terms from now on."

"Maybe you brushed him off because, he's a danger, he might have potential. Perhaps you like being single more than you admit, or maybe you're afraid not to be."

"Well, now look who's Doctor Phil?" Julia laughed, "you're right though, I have to give it some thought."

"Maybe imaginary men are always better than the real thing," Charley offered.

"Robert Downey Junior? George Clooney? Brad Pitt? Those-kind-of-imaginary?"

"Oh yeah, all three of those-kind-of-imaginary."

They bantered back and forth the names of celebrity men they found attractive. It was three hours after Charley first called Julia that Garry slid his key card in and opened the door to find her on her stomach, on the bed, in a red nightshirt he knew had a big white maple leaf on the front, her legs in the air, crossed at the ankles behind her, the plugged-in phone on the bed. She was talking to a woman and they were discussing politics, or something related to it as the voice on the speaker-phone said something about the Prime Minister.

"I can come back after," he offered, and Charley jumped over onto her back, raising her forefinger to tell him to stay.

"Hey, Julia, Garry just got back. I'll call you when I get to Nan's and we'll chat again." It had been hours and her phone hadn't even regained a serious charge. It had also been a blast. Who knew a telephone chat could be so fun?

"Sounds good, enjoy the rest of the trip. I'll keep an eye on things here, no worries," Julia signed off.

Garry noted the empty wine bottle, the discarded KFC box and the empty chip bags.

"You had yourself a party?" he asked, throwing the car keys on the table.

"Just having a chat on the phone with a friend," Charley said, happy.

Garry smiled, surprised but pleased.

For Charley, a conversation like that was a very big deal.

Chapter 28

Charley answered a comment on the previous night's video and then put down her phone. She finally had reliable service again in Parry Sound. Her broadcast had been a lot more fun, she had talked about canoeing, Sleeping Giant and how they were such awful explorers they couldn't see such a huge landmark. She talked of friends and gossip and threw in some jokes about traveling with a man, which was a new experience to her. She also commented she wished she could speak French so all Canadians could participate and if she ever wrote a book it would be translated into both languages.

Garry focused on getting them to their destination, glancing at the map on the dashboard, following the green line until they pulled into the parking lot.

The Bobby Orr Hall of Fame was a bit more than what they had thought it would be. It was part of the Charles W. Stockey Center for the Performing Arts.

"Is it a triangle, is it square?" What is it?" Charley asked as they approached the geometrically unusual building.

"It's architecturally angular," Garry replied, peering up at the building.

"Not what I expected."

"I like it." Garry nodded, satisfied, then he walked around to the back peering out over Georgian bay, the slight wind rippling the waters, the surface bright blue from the cloudless sky's reflection.

Charley joined him there, reaching for his hand, each lost in their thoughts.

After a few moments, she pivoted, letting him go, getting in position to take a photo of the big number four at the top of the facility's sign. One with the good camera, one with the iPhone to send to social media.

"Ready? It's ten, they're open now," she asked when she finished her uploads. He was still staring at the lake.

"Ready Freddy," he said with a grin.

They paid their fee to enter and found themselves surrounded by black and gold.

"They have a statue of the flying shot." Charley snapped a photo before walking up beside it. "This is so cool, wasn't this the greatest hockey moment in history? I think so."

"Paul Anderson goal against the Russians?"

"Nope, can't agree. This was a bigger deal. The Stanley cup is always a bigger deal."

"You're a terrible Canadien's fan you know, defending the Bruins."

"You're a terrible Leafs fan, but then, the leafs are indefensible." She stuck her tongue out.

"Weird how hockey turned out to be our Canadian sport uh?" Garry was looking at the memorabilia," and even the American teams are Canadian because we create the vast majority of the players."

"I think we're only at around 50% now, the other countries are catching up. But it is odd. Ever wonder what sort of guy decided, hey, let's strap blades to our boots and try to move forward on ice on them?"

"Seems like a guy with vision to me."

"Or a fondness for falling on his ass. Perhaps it was a girl?"

"You never know, women come up with crazy ideas too."

"And rarely get credit for the good ones in history."

"Not going to argue that. Hey, look at this." He was pointing to an area where people could participate. It was called "Top Shot" and there were several games they could play.

"Wanna do it?" Charley asked.

"I'll crush this. I played for years."

"You will but that's not the point."

"It's not?"

"Nope, the point is playing, and taking pictures. Go, do it."

So, they shot photos, and Garry wasn't exaggerating, he was a wicked shot, so much so Charley stopped taking a turn to cheer him on. The lights on the square panels illuminated as he hit them.

"This is addictive," Garry said as he left the game, wishing the next player, a young kid around twelve, luck.

"I know, I wasn't very good but you were amazing. Wicked shot. Did you have to give up when you were injured?"

"Yeah, that injury was part of it. Then I sort of fell out of the habit but I think I'd like to play again. I skated last winter. It's fun. Great exercise."

They meandered around, read the signs and left, the drive to Stratford likely to take them four hours counting dinner.

They punched the Bruce Hotel address into the navigation system.

"This takes us down the four hundred, then to a county route, avoiding the 401, is that OK?" Garry asked.

"Oh, yeah, it'll be much nicer to take a rural route. We've done enough big highways, let's go for it."

They drove in companionable silence for a long while, turning off before Barrie onto Ontario Nine west and followed the navigation system's voice as it directed her past rolling green fields, horse ranches, rows upon rows of corn to a left turn at rural route ten and then another after on route 109.

"This is not what I thought Ontario looked like," Charley confessed. First the north with its rocks and forests and now these acres upon acres of rural land.

"It's green and large and really flat."

"Not Saskatchewan level but yeah, incredibly flat."

"We're going dead west, which is strange when you're headed east," Garry remarked looking at the compass on the screen.

"Well we're not going back, just on a detour. And I'm glad we are."

"Me too."

"I have a question for you."

"Yeah?"

"Why couldn't you fly home? You would be there now, settled in."

"Are you sorry I came?"

"Answer the question."

"After Quebec?"

"Forget Quebec." To hell with this, she was getting the answer now.

"I can't fly because…it's a long story." Garry tried to breathe, he wasn't ready to talk about this again. When he had talked about it to his therapist, it had not gone well for him.

"What happened Garry?" Charley lowered her voice. She wanted him to talk, not get angry.

"I don't know. I was fine. I was a good cop. There are things you see when you're a cop that people should never see. There is violence, there are traffic accidents, there are times kids are hurt, it's a difficult job but I was fine."

"Until you got shot?" Charley tried to make it easy, fill in the words.

He nodded his head, his eyes hidden behind his prescription aviator style sunglasses. He stared west, the sky a clear blue, the air conditioner fan blowing on his face to cut the thirty-degree Celsius heat and humidity.

"No. The injury wasn't it," Garry spoke, his voice breaking.

"Tell me Garry," Charley encouraged him.

"I thought I was having a heart attack the first time. I was in the car, on my way from playing hockey, and my partner Rob, drove me to the hospital. They found nothing wrong. They said it was an anxiety attack. I thought it was real, I mean it was painful and it was frightening, and then they started coming regularly. I took leave, I didn't feel like I could do the job well enough, so I decided to take a trip, an all-inclusive trip with this girl I knew. I was kind of seeing her regularly. So, we were on the plane, and we were off to Cancun, four Star resort, all inclusive. And we had a blast, we had a great time, not a problem, but then on the return flight."

"You had a panic attack?"

"Yeah, it was the worse one. I don't know why. I don't know what triggered it but the plane was forced to land, I was removed because they weren't sure if I was sick or if I was dangerous because I freaked out. They were trying to restrain me and I lost it. I don't recall much of it but Sherry—that's the girl—she told me after, right when she said she had to stop seeing me. I rented a car and drove myself back to Vancouver from Seattle where we landed. Christ, I was almost home."

"So, when did you get shot?"

"I didn't *get* shot." Garry hadn't moved, his entire demeanor robotic and emotionless.

"But, you said you did. And you have a wound."

"I became very depressed, the anxiety was unstoppable, I stopped going out, stopped socializing, stopped answering calls. I barely got out of bed." Such a dark time. There hadn't been pain, there hadn't been agony or sadness. It was just numbness and a complete lack of caring if he lived or died.

"I decided if I didn't care if I lived or died, I might as well die. So, I decided to end it all."

"Oh, my God." Charley almost wished she hadn't asked. She could tell he was reliving those times. She reached out, touched him briefly, encouraging him.

"I was interrupted, friends picked up on some clues. Maybe I didn't want to die after all, because there had been hints, and Rob and my ex-girlfriend, Sherry, busted in and stopped me, the gun went off and I was injured but only mildly. I was so pissed at them, and so guilty because either one of them could have been shot."

"And you don't know what triggered this entire thing, what caused the attacks?"

"My therapists say there is often a build-up and the triggering incident might be mild. One of the guys got cut at the hockey game by a skate blade. Maybe that triggered it. Who knows. It was nothing compared to what I've seen when I've been on duty."

"So, you have anxiety attacks and you've had depression?"

"I have depression. I control it with medication. I have taken a lot of steps to recover. I was hospitalized for a while, then I recovered so life felt worth the effort, thanks to a doctor who found me the right drug. That took years. Mental health support sucks in this country. I lived in Vancouver. I'd be dead if I lived in a rural area or up north."

"Years? To find help?"

"To find the help that worked yeah, I had some dark times in those years, the self-loathing, the guilt, the feelings of worthlessness and then the despair of feeling nothing, but I've surfaced and I think I'm on a good path now. So, you see, I couldn't fly home. I can't risk it. What if it happened again?"

"How long since you have had an anxiety attack?"

"It's been years, they stopped pretty much when the depression set in. Yeah, not a good trade off."

"So, you would likely be fine, if you flew I mean?"

"I can't know for sure. What if the plane is the trigger?"

"Want to test that theory? Want to fly?"

"No."

"A tiny plane? With a pilot you know?

"I don't know any pilots."

"You know me. I have a Private Pilot License."

"You're fucking with me?"

"Nope. I really do."

"I am not falling for this, you always get me," he smiled. She was such a joker. It helped that she kidded.

"Okay, don't believe me but if I did, would you fly with me?" She had taken flying lessons when she first moved to British Columbia and still maintained it, flying every so often to keep her skills up to date.

"Absolutely, yep, I'd fly with you."

"Promise?" Perhaps she could rent a plane and take him up, see how things went.

"Pinky-swear promise," and he held up two fingers like a Boy Scout.

"That's not pinky-swear," she laughed, "alright then, I'll rent us a plane in Gander. Oh look, let's get some pictures of that. She pointed to dozen or so horses in a field, with the backdrop of a large red barn, some silos with a windrow of large trees. Charley pulled over and hopped out, grabbing the camera from the back seat.

Garry sat in the car waiting, exhausted from his retelling of his story. She couldn't fly a plane, could she? Nothing about her would surprise him.

There were more details about his life he could have shared like all the times he had lied about his situation, the friendships he had lost due to his unwillingness to go back and explain why he had dropped out of their lives. The copious amounts of booze he'd consumed trying to numb the pain of it all. There were those he had un-friended on social media, and in real life, whose calls and texts he'd ignored. But he was better, the past year a stable one with no dips into that black space, the support of an amazing psychiatrist and a bunch of tools that helped him get through when the odd bout of malaise slipped in. He was also learning to discern what was normal sadness from what was medical depression. And he knew the melancholy he felt at the thought of Charley heading back to Vancouver, while he stayed in Newfoundland, was appropriate, not pathological. He was attached to her and would miss her.

She popped back in the car, her smile the same as before he had told her his story. Had he expected her to change somehow?

"Ready for Bieberland? Let's go Han Solo," she said.

"I'll never be ready for Bieber, but let's go Charley," he laughed, relieved at how normal things remained.

She flicked the entertainment button and selected a song. "*Is it too late now to say sorry,*" the song piped into the van and she danced with it, driving them towards Stratford and the next adventure.

Chapter 29

"Do you know what I love about Canada?" Charley exited Twitter, shaking her head.

"Everything?" Garry guessed.

"No not everything but this kind of thing. There is a guy in Waterloo, who, in celebration of Canada's 150th birthday built a tower out of hundreds of Tim Horton's cups."

"Really?"

"Yep, saw it on Twitter, he set up a Go-Fund-Me, promoted through twitter, raised money to buy coffees for people then reclaimed the cups. There are pictures. Also, there is a Tim Horton's Hashtag full of people doing selfies with their cups."

"That's a bit out there." Garry shook his head, reading some of the tweets.

"It's fun. This is a nice room uh? Only one night here because semolians. Lots of semolians."

"What are semolians?"

"Dollars, moolah."

"Never heard that word before. But it's appropriate. It cost me a lot of semolians but I bought us tickets for *Romeo and Juliet* tonight at 8pm, wear your best theater duds, because I've moved our date up to tonight. Since I've spilled the beans about my secrets and you didn't threaten to drop me at Union Station in Toronto, I decided you deserve a treat. And, we also have tickets for a two O'clock matinee for *Guys and Dolls* tomorrow, I figure we can check out and then take in the show, before heading east again. Sound good?" He waited. It was the first time he had made plans for them.

"Yes!" Charley shouted. "I get to dress up? I'm going shopping, they have nice stores along Ontario Street, and we can walk down by the water and see the famous Stratford Swans."

"This is the nicest hotel room I've ever stayed at. I'm glad we splurged." Garry wandered around, running a hand along the furniture, checking out the fresh fruit and flowers.

"YOLO, right?" he added. You only live once. His savings were taking a dent but hell this was a great trip.

"Yep, definitely YOLO. So, we will do this fancy date in Stratford. I'm in. Thou dost well to spoil me William," she said in a bad Elizabethan accent.

"Forsooth," he answered.

They strolled the trail that encircled the Avon River, poked fun at the names of the streets, all Shakespeare themed. But while they pretended it was all a bit contrived, they couldn't help but get caught up in the beauty of the small theater town. There was a horse and buggy offering rides and they jumped on and learned all sorts of trivia, like the fact Thomas Edison once lived in a room on Grange Street while he worked for a short time as a telegraph operator. The driver also pointed out the stairs where Bieber had busked.

"Garry loves Justin Bieber," Charley gushed to the people in the carriage with them.

"He's my very *fave*," Garry responded, putting his arm around her and giving a little squeal.

Charley stuck her tongue out at him and cuddled closer, holding his hand.

The pretty town was equally famous for its Shakespearian festival, the largest outside of the real Stratford-Upon-Avon, home of the Bard himself. The city was abloom with flowers and several dragon boats practiced, the teams in perfect rhythm as they shot through the water with precision at a shout from their coach.

"They're better than we were with the canoe." Charley licked the chocolate off a cone purchased at *Jenn and Larry's Brittles and Shakes*, a local ice cream & sweets parlour tucked away in a little alley off the main street. Garry disagreed allowing they were far better coordinated and united in their strokes than the team of twenty or so that came to a halt near a pedal boat rental place.

"We have time to rent one. Wanna go for a spin?" Charley asked, "then we'll go look for something for me to wear later."

"Deal, though I like what you're wearing today." Her white tank top was snug around her breasts and her red shorts were the shortest she had ever worn. She had a slight tan line below the shorts but her legs were strong and fit and her hair was in a ponytail, tucked through the hole at the back of a white baseball hat. She was still wearing red and white, still strong with the Canadian colours.

They rolled along in the paddle boat, side by side, bright orange life vests over their shirts. A larger boat full of tourists passed them and they waved, smiled and carried on.

They moved forward, the large Festival Theater coming into sight, the heat of the day melting them so their paddling was lazy and slow.

"This is wonderful. It is relaxing, beautiful, serene, even though it's busy and crowded. Everybody is in a good mood."

"We've come a long way Orlando Bloom."

"What? What happened to Indiana Jones and Han Solo? Or William Shakespeare even?"

"You've been upgraded."

"Why Orlando Bloom?"

"He is British, he was in Romeo and Juliet and he's hot. Stay with me Clark Kent."

"You're nuts."

"We should not joke about mental illness. You know there is a great stigma attached which we must remove."

Garry laughed. Her jokes took the edge of his own fears about judgment. If they could joke about this, there wasn't much to be afraid of.

"You are right, my apologies, carry on." He did a sort of seated flourish and a bow as though he were an actor himself.

"Thanks. As I was saying, we've come a long way Orlando Bloom," she shot him a side eye before continuing, "and I've come to one conclusion about this country."

"That is?" He let her paddle as they turned around.

"There are no conclusions. It's a weird combination of circumstance and deliberate creation. We define it one way, others define it another, but we all kind of get along for the most part."

"And it's safe. It is seriously safe. We are in Ontario, the biggest province and there is no general danger of any kind. There aren't a lot of places can say that," he responded.

Charley spoke, thoughtful. "I remember one time, the battery died in my car when I was in Vancouver. I'd been there for a parade. I posted on my Facebook I needed a boost, left my car, walked into a restaurant, came out and waited for a local tow truck. All bored and alone, I checked my Facebook and there was a somber warning from a friend of mine who lived near Detroit that advised me to please stay safe. Meanwhile, it had never once crossed my mind there was any possibility of danger. It was a mere inconvenience. But in considering it I thought, yeah, if I broke down in Detroit, I'd be nervous. Maybe I shouldn't be but there is a sense of danger there I don't feel here. Is there a single city in Canada where you would be afraid if you broke down, needed a boost at 8pm at night? I can't think of one. Some areas are worse than others but I can't think of one."

"Neighbourhoods I suppose but no, I've engaged in conversations with American law enforcement people and they're in a whole other sort of business. They're often in survival mode, we're in serve and protect. It's different."

"We're also white, and you're a male and a cop. Maybe we're not the best judges of how safe this country is. If I were an indigenous woman, it's a fact, I wouldn't be as safe."

"That is a sobering fact," Garry agreed.

They paddled back towards the rental place, and made their way to Ontario Street so Charley could find something suitable for the theater. It was easy, there were several stores selling nice dresses and she found something she liked and a pair of shoes to match.

Gone was the red and white. She stood before the full-length mirror checking out her reflection. The periwinkle blue spaghetti-strap gown fell over her slender frame, the fabric shimmery, comfortable, fitted and revealing. It stopped just above her knees. Her tanned legs slid into high wedge shoes and large gold hoops and a white pashmina completed the look. The scarf, pretty and classic, could be used as a wrap if the theater was chilly.

Garry came in, and gave a low whistle. "Wow," he said.

He looked pretty spiffy himself, dappered-out in a grey suit and tie, the facial hair that sprouted on the trip gone, his glasses replaced by contact lenses. It was a Clarke Kent transformation that stopped her dead in her tracks.

"Holy crap, you clean up good Superman," she quipped, giving a low whistle right back.

"And you look beautiful, but you always do," he replied.

"Thank you." She turned back to the mirror adjusting her long straight dark hair, checking her subtle makeup, adding a tad more lipstick.

"I need to get one thing straight though, before we go okay?" Garry said.

He went over to her and she turned around. He looked down into her eyes, his expression serious.

"Superman's an upgrade from Orlando Bloom, right?"

"You figure it out sunshine," she laughed, leading the way out the door.

Chapter 30

Charley settled back into her chair in *The Restaurant* at The Bruce Hotel, the perfect table set with bright white linens and sparkling silverware. A near-empty bottle of chilled wine leaned into its cradle, the remnants of their dessert on their plates. All was whisked away by a waiter moments after they finished, their wine glasses and their bellies both full.

"I could get used to this." Charley glanced around, satiated from the six courses. They had ordered from the tasting menu, enjoying bits of nearly everything the restaurant offered, savouring every morsel. The food was fresh, locally foraged and sourced. A delight for any palate.

"I want to do this every day, that was good."

"We'll have hamburgers tomorrow, Chewbacca." She glanced at her phone. "We have time to walk to the theater." She finished her wine, and rolled her eyes with pleasure.

"You know the names you keep randomly calling me make no sense, right?"

"Of course not, if they made sense then you would predict them, and I can't be predictable now can I?"

"No, I would never predict you would be." He winked as he handed a credit card to the waiter, a nice tip added to the total.

"I feel bad though, I'm going to have to budget my way through the east coast. We won't be contributing to the economy quite so much down there, this room cost the equivalent of several Holiday Inn nights."

"But well worth it." He poked his credit card into his wallet and stood, coming around to pull her chair out and she stood. Then, tucking her arm into the crook of his, he made a big show of gentlemanly chivalry.

"Not bad, Bruce Wayne," she said, walking beside him along the river. The sun was still warm on their backs. She was up past his shoulders in the high wedge shoes. A dozen swans lazed along the shore, cygnets trailing behind a solo mother following along as they walked towards the Festival Theater.

"Have you ever seen Romeo and Juliet?" Charley asked him as they settled into their seats.

"No, haven't even read it. Know something of the story, teenagers, feuding families, suicide and so on. Tragic stuff."

"Sara Farb, Antoine Yared, Marion Adler..." Charley read the cast in a low voice.

"Oh, does that mean it's starting?" A trumpet had sounded, reminiscent of the period in which the play was set.

"I think so!" Charley tucked the program in her purse as the lights went down and the orchestra hit its first notes.

"Hope I understand what is happening. I don't speak Shakespeare."

"You will, you're a smart guy," she shifted a little, whispering in his ear, "nice date so far Romeo"

He took her hand and smiled in the dark.

The following morning, they lounged in bed, nursing mild headaches from the wine consumed in large amounts at the restaurant, the theater and then later in the room. The van was packed by checkout.

They stood at the desk, taking care of the details when a fuss was made over a young woman who entered the lobby with a baby in a carrier. Charley couldn't help but be taken by the little guy who laughed and stole her heart.

The pretty young mom explained how she had worked here until he was born and would be back after her maternity benefits expired when he was a year old.

Not having had a family herself, she hadn't given much consideration to the way Canada was for families. In an abstract way, she knew there were supports.

She asked the young mother her thoughts.

The young woman explained that with her income it might not be worthwhile to return to her job, childcare being so expensive. They might qualify for a subsidy but it was a real problem. Her co-workers understood, having lost several employees to the issue. The young woman, Christie, explained she wanted to work, that if she lost this job she lost future income as well. Charley pondered this as she joined Garry at the desk. She had found the topic for her next blog post.

They ate burgers at Boomers, a local joint, skipping breakfast altogether. After the show, they headed east once more, checking into a hotel in Montreal at midnight.

Garry registered them, Charley understanding none of the French beyond *comment all-overs* or some such thing.

"I don't know what you said to that guy but that's impressive. I wish I had learned."

"My New Brunswick family was bilingual and I made a point of speaking it so I wouldn't lose it. I practiced it as much as I could. We had French-Canadian officers wherever I worked, always found it odd that people don't realize that there are Francophones all over this country."

"I know. Hey, do you know the lady who sang *The French Song*, was from out in BC, a Francophone settlement out there?"

"I do know it. Head to the room, I'll be right up. Going to grab something else from the van."

A few moments after Charley arrived in the room, Garry showed up with his guitar case.

"I nearly forgot you had a guitar with you. They rarely had to open the back of the van since leaving British Columbia, their necessary items all in the back seat.

"Yep, think it's too late to play one little song?"

"Nope, do it."

Garry tuned a bit, his fingers nimble as he flicked the keys and strings, strumming and listening. He gave it several more strums, nodded, satisfied then started in on the well-known tune.

Quand le soleil dit bonjour aux montagnes,
Et que la nuit rencontre le jour.

Je sui seule avec mes reves sur la montagne,

Une voix me rapelle toujours.

Ecoute a ma porte les chansons du vent,

237

M'rapelle les souvenirs de toi

Quand le soleil dit bonjour aux montagnes

Je suis seule, je ne veux penser qu'a toi

When the sun says good-day to the mountains

And the night says hello to the dawn

I'm alone with my dreams on the hilltop

And I can still hear his voice though he's gone

I hear from my door the love songs through the wind

It brings back sweet memories of you.

Quand le soleil dit bonjour aux montagnes

Je suis seule, je ne veux penser qu'a toi.

His soft voice filled the room, the light guitar music accompanying it.

"I love this. I've always thought this was such a pretty song."

"First song ever to sell a million copies, Lucille Starr, a Francophone from Coquitlam."

"Sing it again." Charley was entranced by both the song and his voice.

"Sing it with me."

"I'll sing the English bits with you," she agreed.

They spent another half an hour singing then tucked in for the night, holding each other in the hotel bed. The lights off, the sounds of traffic, the rattle of the air conditioner and the glow of a bathroom light keeping Charley awake longer than she intended.

She was going to have to pull back a bit, this guy was getting under her skin. She was getting too attached, liking too much the feel of him holding her, of having a companion to do things like sing songs with her.

She pulled away, turning her back to him as his steady breath marked the moments until she slipped into a restless sleep, alone, on her own side of the bed.

Chapter 31

Enraptured, they toured the city of Quebec.. There was, for Charley, something exotic about everybody around her speaking French, and being alone in her English brain.

Garry spanned the language barrier with ease, asking questions, repeating answers, impressing her with his capacity to flip back and forth between the two.

"How good is your French? Compared to your English I mean?" Charley was in the passenger seat, they were headed to The Shrine of Sainte-Anne-de-Beaupré.

"It's as good as my English, vocabulary-wise but I do have a slight accent. I started learning it late. My mother was perfectly bilingual. You couldn't tell which was her first language."

"Nice. When I get back home to BC I'm going to learn."

"I'll be happy to help you, we can chat in French. It's the easiest way to pick up a language. Just talk in that language all the time."

"You won't be there."

"I mean on Skype or by phone." He stared straight ahead, reading the signs.

"I am not a big Skype or phone chatter, plus once the school year starts I don't have much free time to socialize. After this trip is over I doubt we'll talk much at all."

"No, I suppose not." Garry pulled into the parking lot and turned off the ignition, pocketing the keys. The van was once more packed for the road, their only planned side trip, two night's in Prince Edward Island, otherwise it was Irving Stations and driving until North Sydney."

"Oh, my God, this place is gorgeous." The Basilica was in the shape of a cross, somewhere around sixty meters wide and at least a hundred meters in length. It was equally as high as it was long if you measured to the top of the bell tower Charley estimated. She relayed her guesses and Garry agreed.

"It feels, I don't know, might sound weird, but it *feels* holy," Garry said. He walked beside her as they entered the sanctuary, its large Romanesque Revival architecture impressive and awe inspiring.

The bas-relief of the facade displayed Saint Anne. At either side of their feet, a frieze represented historical moments. There were angels, the twelve apostles, statues of Mary, John the Baptist, and others by a Québec sculptor, Émile Brunet.

The statue of Sainte Anne had once been saved from a fire that destroyed the first basilica in 1922. They walked in silence, taking in the entirety of the shrine.

"It does feel holy, and I'm not even Catholic," Charley agreed.

"I am. But that doesn't have much to do with it. It just feels like it's divine."

"I know what you mean."

"After my episode, my injury," Garry cleared his throat, "I would go regularly to the Holy Rosary Cathedral in Vancouver and sit. I didn't pray, but it was so peaceful, and I could feel it was healing in some way. Sometimes there would be Nuns praying at the front of the church and I would sit in the back and watch them. They would pray for hours, they were there when I arrived and there, still as the dead, when I left."

"I'm all about tossing up the short little devotion for a friend, but spending hours in prayer is a good waste of the time we have."

"Well, we all waste time. Between television, social media and stuff, but if you're doing what makes you happy, what fulfills you, then I guess it's not a waste."

"I think television is a huge waste of time. Social media has value but most people don't know how to use it properly. But alone, in a church, praying, instead of out, in the community, doing. Well that's wasteful. Does God need, long drawn out pleas repeated over and over? Or would a simple, hey God, Tommy needs new shoes, help him find a way, be as effective. Especially if you search for sales, toss it on your credit card, and buy the shoes for poor Tommy."

"Oh, I agree. But that doesn't mean sitting in that church, with those silent ladies, didn't sooth my heart when it needed soothing. And that's as important as shoes. Shoes, for me back then, were easy to come by. Solace, not so much."

"I'm glad it helped. And I'll keep it in mind. I'm not a church-goer but if I ever find myself wanting some comfort I won't rule it out as a possibility.

They left the basilica, and headed back to the car.

"Do you want to go to the Mosque in Ste-Foy? Garry asked.

"Yes, I need to pay respects."

A short while later they stood before the Islamic Cultural Center.

"I don't know quite what I'm supposed to say or think about this," she said.

The massacre by a crazed extreme nationalist terrorist with a gun fascination, allegedly inspired by the right-wing government of the United States had killed six people and injured more while they prayed. It had shocked and united much of the country against such hatred.

"Donate? I felt so helpless back then I did the only thing I could."

"I didn't, I'm embarrassed to say, but I will." She took his hand.

"I don't feel it's appropriate we go in or stay too long, do you?"

"No, I don't want to be a gawker, I can feel the trauma, it must be so raw to the people who come here. We were just then at a cathedral where we felt so incredibly in awe, in a sense of peace. And imagine if something like this had happened while we were there. That's how it happened for these people." She took one last look before they strolled back to the van, heads down, sad.

"Worse, we were merely tourists," Garry replied, "we weren't congregants, praying. It is very tragic."

They were silent for quite a long while after, lost in their thoughts. Somber and troubled.

"We can make Fredericton in six hours. Find us a place?" Charley spoke first trying to shake the dark mood.

"Do we have a plan beyond Fredericton?" Garry was relieved to think of something else.

"Nah, I figure we'll take it one Irving at a time Jean Pierre," she grinned.

"Vous êtes la femme la plus folle que j'ai jamais rencontrée Charlotte Andrews," Garry said.

"Wait, what? What does that mean?"

"I said you look pretty with your hair down."

"No, you didn't." She shot him a glare from the driver's seat.

"Prove it Celine," he cracked, and rubbed his bicep where she whacked him a second later.

"Off to New Brunswick," Charley declared, setting the car in drive and pulling out.

Chapter 32

Garry tossed the flat tire into the van, the new one in place. The black night required it to be changed by the light of Charley's phone flashlight, her curse words at the first wobble still hung in the air somewhere a few miles back.

"What a friggin' pain," she grumbled as they crested the hill.

"Chips?" Garry pointed to the bag and she pinched a few between her fingers and thumb, stuffing them in.

"Think we'll get anything to eat? Anything open?" They would have arrived in Fredericton late but had lost another hour with the flat, having to unpack the entire trunk in the dark to get to the spare. Then pack it back up again, making sure the busted tire was at the top so they could get it repaired before leaving in the morning.

"Yeah, we will. We're pretty lucky that was the only thing that happened. Hey, what are those lights?"

"Looks like laser beams." She did air quotes around "laser" as if she were Mike Myers in an Austin Powers move, mimicking how he said the word.

"Yeah, baby," Garry's impersonation of the international man of mystery impeccable.

"Wait, the Aurora Borealis? Northern lights? In July?"

"I thought they were only in the winter?"

"That's the only time I've seen them. But then I saw them in the north where it was mostly winter."

"I haven't seen them since I was a child but that most definitely is them."

They drove towards the dancing green flickers, their intense colours getting brighter on their approach. The kaleidoscope of green with flashes of pink raised high towards the stars, then bounced down and back up higher and higher, spreading the breadth of the horizon, a performance of such splendour and beauty both Charley and Garry were silent for half an hour, hunger sated with salt and vinegar chips and some OMGs Clusters.

The radio play list was still on shuffle, familiar voices taking turns filling the time as the travelers marveled at the atmospheric spectacle of the Aurora Borealis. Jim Cuddy's voice broke through Charley's thoughts, one of her favourite songs by Blue Rodeo spinning an appropriate lament to the situation she found herself in.

Maybe soon there'll be a time, when no more tears will fall, we'll both look back on it, cry a little bit, bad timing is all.

"We've got bad timing, don't we?" Garry echoed her thoughts, eyes straight ahead, the beauty of the night sky mesmerizing, lulling him into sentimentality and somehow, sadness.

"The worse. We're headed in different directions, though right now it's like we're not." She flicked the lights in high beam for no real reason but habit.

"No chance you'll stay in the province?" Garry knew the answer.

"Nope, not staying, my life is in BC. I've a lot going on back there. And you've got to get yourself together, figure out your life. We're both adults, we're hardly in love in that short a time, it's been a nice trip, we've had some fun, still can have some fun, we'll be in Prince Edward Island tomorrow, at the ferry in a couple of days. We're almost through Canada and it's been great."

"We could have fallen in love though, with more time. I could see that." Garry's feelings were strong, he liked her and could see them being happy together but she was right, it was definitely too soon for anything serious. And they were running out of time, running out of Canada.

"Let's enjoy what's left of it okay? Let's forget the serious stuff Han Solo, let's travel through, see Green Gables and the red roads of PEI, then on to Cape Breton, then home sweet home." Her voice was perky, too much so. *Fallen in love.* Wow.

"You're still having fun? You seem anxious to get there now, not so into the journey."

"I'm like a horse."

"You're a horse now? How are you like a horse? I'd like to think I'm like a horse—" He winked and eyed her with a leer.

"Woah boy, you have nothing to be ashamed of but stallion you are not," she laughed.

"I'm hurt." His fake wounded-look had her laughing more.

"You'll live," she responded, "and what I mean is, my grandfather used to have a horse for hauling wood back when he was a boy. So, he would always say this," she reverted to her Newfoundland dialect, "a horse will trot along, on the way to the woods, a nice slow pace, then you spends the day cutting wood, loading it on the sled and he'll start to trudge back, right slow. But then, t'ree parts of the way he'll take off like 'is tail is on fire, he can smell home and when he gets close, he gives 'er, because there is nothing like home. For nobody."

"Yeah, I guess. I've been stationed all over so I haven't had a permanent home. Nan is drawing me back, but it would be nice to have a place to draw me. I need a change of scenery, to get away from the city. You have two places. Or is Bowen Island not like that for you?"

"It is. I'm anxious to get to my first island now. It is home. Always will be. But I haven't been there in so long, well, most of what I know of it is nostalgia. The bad stuff has faded away. It never was too bad there, that's not where I lived when I had trouble. But, I've made a new place for myself. My house is not fancy but I like the way the kitchen catches the sun. Love my shelves of books, the tiny gifts lined up on them, from the students. I think I might get a cat when I get back, share it. I've a few grey hairs now, which I'll never colour so my crazy cat lady days are getting close. God, I think those lights are getting brighter."

"Yeah, they are. Looks like they're dancing. Nature gives us so many gifts uh? I love music but nothing makes my heart sing like a still lake, a raging ocean or the northern lights."

"You're a bit of a poetic soul aren't you Garry Clarke?"

"That's my real name, are you ill?" He placed his hand tenderly over her forehead and she swatted it away.

"Shut up. I can be serious at times you know."

"Yeah, I know, you're a bit too serious some times. We're closing in on the city, you're about two exits away from the motel."

"Great I could use a good night's sleep."

"Food first, pizza? I could order ahead, we could grab it and then go to the hotel."

"Works for me John Boy."

"You're fucked up," he stated.

"So royally, yeah." He had no idea, she thought.

Chapter 33

They crossed the Confederation Bridge, spanning the Abegweit Passage of the Northumberland Straight at eleven in the morning, tire repaired. They toured the Anne of Green Gables Museum a few hours later.

Charley and Garry wandered through the grounds, the red roads winding around the property and Charlotte was mesmerized by the green fields, with its bright blossoms, imagining her childhood heroine flitting around the property, alive and happy, though she never had existed. Garry was amused to see the childlike glee she took in her surroundings, listening as she regaled him with Anne trivia, talked herself into buying a hard copy of the book, and out of buying herself an Anne doll.

"I always wanted an Anne doll," she confessed, stroking the red braids of the twenty-inch replica of the fictional character sitting at a wooden desk, tiny slate with a crack in it. But she moved on and grabbed the book instead.

"You should get it." Charlotte hadn't purchased a thing on the trip except the dress in Stratford.

"Nah, I'll get the book, it'll be nice to show the class. Makes more sense." She headed to the till, then popping her change into her camera bag, led him to the van.

"Are you shooting your broadcast here? I can get out of your hair if you like."

"I was going to go a farm, find potato fields to shoot from."

"You go on and do that, I'm going to make some phone calls. How about you swing back and pick me up when you're done?"

"Sounds good. Need anything from the van?"

He grabbed his backpack while she settled in the driver's seat. "Got it," he replied before she set off.

She didn't have to drive far to find a potato field and at the end of the lane, near a large barn she located the farmer. She was glad Garry wasn't with her. She had an idea for today's broadcast she wanted to be a surprise for him. It was about him, a serious topic.

She introduced herself to the farmer, his soft island accent and genuine smile warmer than the Cavendish sun.

"Sure, you can do your Facebook thing, we got WiFi up here near the house, you can pick it up at the barn so you should be fine."

"I can hot spot to my phone, cell service is good here too." Charley noted the full number of bars.

"Not everybody has it but we're wired up here! No password, nobody close enough to sign on anyway."

She logged into their WiFi and said, "thank you so much, this is great, you mind if I go over there by the tractor? I can set up so the field is behind me."

"You do whatever you like. I'm going to get Jessie, the wife, to add you on her Facebook so she can see what you do."

"Thanks, more people the better!"

Charlotte hoisted her camera bag upon the large wheel of the tractor, positioned her iPad and tapped her Facebook App. The WiFi registered with full bars from there as well. The potatoes with their green leaves, divided in rows, the red soil perfect straight lines between them, gave her a lush backdrop for her five minutes.

She knew what she was going to say, the words in her head as she drove away from the museum. Garry had inspired the topic.

"Hello Canadians! It's Charley here again, checking in on the Charley Does Canada tour! Today I'm here in glorious Prince Edward Island, at the farm of Lyle Campbell, and behind me is a huge potato field. It's looking to be a bumper year for spuds. We are about to leave to cross back over the bridge, heading to Nova Scotia but you know I had to do my little broadcast, loving the sound of my own voice as I do. That's for you, ONYX975469 who commented I did, on my last broadcast. Yes, I do like the sound of my own voice. It's been a gift, something I can use to help others so, I love the sound of it, you caught me. Now enough about you, this broadcast is all about me!" She smiled into the camera as the laughing smileys floated across the screen. She carried on with her monologue.

"As you can see this is a beautiful spot in this great big country. I just came from touring the Anne of Green Gables Museum, which is why I'm wearing the braids and this straw hat today." She pointed to her head.

"I've learned so much already, like how on July 22, 1883 a three-masted world record-holding Clipper Ship grounded and broke up on Cavendish Beach. So, if you go to a beach and find a bunch of kids playing Marco Polo, you might wonder if that's where the game was invented. I don't know if that's true but Marco Polo is the ship and it was lost, not far from here.

So, today's main topic isn't about fun and games and it isn't small potatoes either. Okay, even

I groaned at that." She shook her head, carrying on, her smiled changing to a more serious expression.

"It's a big and important topic and one we all need to think about and take action on. As you know, I've a companion on this trip who wishes to remain off-screen but I feel perhaps it's time to talk about bit more about him. First off, he is former RCMP officer, and since this is my journey across Canada in celebration of our country, he is a very appropriate companion."

She cleared her throat.

"Second, we have had some good conversations, and one in particular has me thinking about an issue in this country that needs addressing and it is that of mental health support. My companion has been battling with some issues, and in the not-so-distant past he has suffered depression and anxiety and has come close to dying because of it, his despair so deep, he attempted to take his own life. Lucky for all of us, he has improved and driving across the country with him, getting to know him, I'm grateful this man has been able to recover but he didn't do it alone, he had help. But the problem is, not everybody can get help. Sometimes those who attempt suicide succeed. Mental illness kills people. If everybody was dying from diabetes because there wasn't medical care, there would be an outrage. Plus some types of mental illness have a physical component and often *is* a physical illness. There are things that can help such as medicine and therapy but it needs to be available to everybody. There is hope and while this country isn't perfect, where it is successful is in making progress."

The little eye on the screen indicated over a thousand people were watching the video and the little thumbs indicated they liked what she was saying. The comments were rolling in and they were all in favour of more supports for people who suffered. She had struck a chord.

"Let's make progress on this. Support of those who serve us is vital, such as in the RCMP and the Military, but also for the regular folk who need assistance. And we must get support immediately to our First Nations communities. Some of them are vastly under-serviced, often with tragic consequences. The first step for sufferers is seeking help. There is a crisis number and I've included it in the description of this broadcast. The first step for the rest of us is to call our representative. As you know, I've a list of their names on my website. There is a link below, email your MP, tell him you want there to be better mental health services for people. I don't pretend to know a lot about this topic but I do know something about compassion and empathy. I've had people treat me well when I needed it most. And it's something all of us can do now. We can stop ourselves short when we're about to judge somebody who suffers with mental illness and instead pivot to compassion and help end the stigma so people are willing to look for help. We can also advocate for those unable to do so themselves. We can do much better."

She paused for a moment, breathing deeply, looking straight into the camera and finishing up. She smiled again, her face showing her pleasure. "Before I go, I do want to give a plug for the Anne of Green Gables Museum, not that they need it because that place was packed with tourists. I wonder, was ever a fictional character so beloved? She was so real in my life as a child that as an adult I forget she wasn't, but then, being fictional doesn't mean she isn't real, right? And while we have problems to fix, calls to make, emails to send on an important topic we still have much to be grateful for. Thank you for joining me today, I see a few thousand of you have tuned in and I'll read all your comments later. But for now, I think it appropriate that, on a sun-shiny day, in a potato field in Prince Edward Island I will end this with a quote from my darling Anne Shirley, *'Dear old world, you are very lovely, and I'm glad to be alive in you.'* Thank-you Prince Edward Island, you are a gem. See you in Nova Scotia! Canadians!"

"God, this place is beautiful," she said to no one as she drew her bag from atop the tire and tucked in the iPad, closing the zip. Mr. Campbell and his wife were down over the steps and met her by the van.

"I've been watching you drive across the country," Jessie Campbell said, her voice deep and husky. "That was wonderful. I lost my brother to suicide when I was seventeen, he was only nineteen. He was troubled his whole life." Her eyes welled and Charley was silent, coming face to face with someone directly affected by the topic she spoke on catching her by surprise.

"I'm so sorry." She reached out and pulled the woman in for a hug, her own tears a breath away from falling.

"I hope nobody else has to go through what my family did, we need to learn a lot about this. I'm going to write that email and when I tell people from here to do it too they will. I don't know if it'll help."

"She will too," her husband chimed in. "When Jess gets something in her head, she gets it done and people will do what she says." There was a certain pride in his declaration.

"It will not hurt, but silence does.Let me know how it goes, here is my card. You email me and let me know OK?"

"I will for sure, say hello to your boyfriend. Tell him I hope he continues to recover."

"Yep, will do."

They hugged again and parted and Charlotte made her way back to Green Gables, happy she seemed to have done something worthwhile. Such a complex issues and she knew her little broadcast was a small contribution. But she felt good about it , and she couldn't wait to tell Garry.

He was waiting, his tall frame unmistakable even in the midst of the crowds that still streamed into the grounds. He didn't speak, climbing in, tossing his backpack in the back. He appeared distracted, taking forever to organize his bag. Maybe she'd wait to tell him on the ferry.

Charley smiled. "Did you get all your calls made?"

"Yeah, did you get your stuff done?"

Charley nodded a yes."Ready for Nova Scotia Jesse James?"

"Ready Dwayne Eddy," he winked.

"How long have you waited to use that?" She gave him a broad grin.

"I thought of it last night," he confessed, laughing.

It was a sound she was starting to like a tad too much.

Chapter 34

Charley should have been happier. Her excitement at going home again was dampened by the realization she had enjoyed this trip so much and would miss Garry like crazy when it was over. She covered by talking about boring things.

"I'm going to do the final broadcast from North Sydney tomorrow, our crossing is at 11:45pm. I'd like to head out early, see a bit of Cape Breton, do the live stream and then get to the ferry terminal. I can't believe we're almost there. It seemed to go so fast after we got through Quebec."

"The Atlantic provinces are much smaller. Have you been talking to your grandmother today? Nan called something like five times. But it's late there now, I don't think I should call back until the morning. She goes to bed at ten sharp and doesn't turn the phone off. I haven't checked in for a few days. Plus, it's even later there. But I don't want her worrying."

"I was talking to Nan for a bit when you were in the shower so she will tell your Grandmother we're fine. And she'll know if anything is wrong with her so I say you're safe to wait."

"Okay, perfect." He climbed into bed and she moved close to him, his warmth, the touch of his chest against her back lending her solace.

Lend was the right word. They were on borrowed time. She had never realized how important touch was because she had gone without it for so long, on purpose, because there had not been much gentle touch in her adult life. Now though, she had grown accustomed to a warm body next to hers, the accidental brushing as they crossed paths in the hotel room, a gentle hand in the crook of her back. She made a point of returning the gestures, though in a somewhat tentative manner. A tap on his thigh, leaning her head against his arm as they sat together or touching his hand across a table. Surely if she needed touch, he did too.

Cape Breton's scenery gave them a sample of what they were in store for in Newfoundland. The rocks jutting into the ocean, the cliffs and hills alive with berry blossoms and burgeoning swamps, evergreens packed in tight forests for kilometers and the same moose-warning signs they had encountered all through the Atlantic provinces.

"The farmer, where I shot my video, told me there are no bears or moose on Prince Edward Island."

"Really? Well there are a lot here." They were in Cape Breton Highlands National Park. Her pass for free admission to the National Parks sat in the window, the best freebie she had gotten in years, even better than the lifetime supply of President's Choice Cookies she had won in a fundraiser a few years back.

Dark and deep, balsam fir and white birch made up most trees in the forest. The Boreal, under threat both in northern Canada and here on the island where the spruce bud worm had destroyed many of the balsams and the overabundance of moose had destroyed the regrowth. That information inspired Charley and she decided the broadcast from Nova Scotia would be about the environment. It was a broad topic, but an important one. The cities had been fun but the best portions of this entire trip had been the untouched nature of the country, the mountains, the lakes, the forests and now, the ocean.

They checked in two hours before their scheduled crossing. Charley did her Facebook Live broadcast, encouraging people to be mindful of waste, of their natural environment, to look to their own communities, see what was worth conserving. Her viewership was triple what it was for her first and her notifications now indicated her page had hit one hundred and twenty-thousand likes, several thousand coming after her Prince Edward Island broadcast.

The wind cooled her face as she made her way back to the van, pleased with her final report, happy the terminal had been quiet enough to record in.

Hopping in the driver seat, her smile halted at the look on Garry's face.

"What happened? What's wrong?" Her heart picked up speed, a strange, noose-like feeling strangled her and she backed up against the door.

"How fucking-dare you? How dare you? Everything I told you regarding my life, was in confidence, and you went and broadcasted it to the world."

"What? I…"

"Shut up, just shut up. Nan told me, and I watched it myself, thousands of people saw what you said. Nobody knew any of that? Do you know that nobody knew, except Nan? And her best friend, your grandmother. They didn't tell you, did they? I did, I trusted you. I can't believe I was so stupid."

"But I didn't, I mean nobody knows who you are." She recoiled from his anger.

"You're not fucking stupid, Charley. You've got thousands of followers, they're all loving your quirky little cross-country tour, you've tapped into the people, have them all excited, and now you've told them I had mental issues and tried to kill myself. The entire damn country knows this, do you think when I step off the ferry on Change Islands they won't figure it out? They're all following you, they love the local girl, getting famous on Facebook for her great trip."

"I never thought of that." Oh shit. He was wrong. She *was* fucking stupid.

"You never thought of me. You never thought of keeping the things I've told you to yourself. I never open up to people, this was private, and you told the entire God-damned country."

"I'm sorry, it wasn't, I didn't mean to..." Charley's tears started then. A familiar self-loathing swept over her. She deserved all the words he was hammering at her and she deserved his hatred because she had been stupid, she had betrayed him and she should have either asked, or not done it.

"I'm going to see if I can walk on with this ticket. I'll find a ride across the island somewhere. Pop the god-damned trunk," he ordered.

She obeyed. What the hell had she done? She was paralyzed as he pulled his stuff out of the back seat then the trunk, making his way across the parking lot towards a worker.

She wanted to run after him, beg him, stop him. But she knew it would do no good.

She didn't see him later when she pulled the van aboard the ferry, nor when she found the cabin where they were both to sleep. His empty bunk remained that way. She didn't know if he was on the ferry or had been required to stay overnight in the terminal and she was terrified to find out.

The ferry lurched out from the wharf at the scheduled time while Charley toss in her bed, sleep evading her. The engine's drone lulled her into a restless doze about an hour before they docked in Newfoundland and when they were all mustered to go to the lower deck in the morning there was still no sign of Garry. She disembarked into Channel-Port Au Basque, tired and distraught, driving across the windy highway until she was required to fill up her gas tank in Corner Brook.

"He's fine," her Nan consoled a weeping Charley. "He called Ger, he was on the ferry and he found somebody coming to Lewisporte, she's going to pick him up from there."

"I thought I was keeping him anonymous, I feel so bad. "She wiped her eyes. She needed to pull herself together. She just felt so damned awful.

"I know love, and while I understand why he's angry, it was just a mistake. Now don't get upset but the media found out who he is, the word got out, it's taken off, people are talking about it, I heard the Prime Minister acknowledged it even. This may make some real change in people lives so Garry might be mad but his story resonated."

"Oh God, Nan that's not good. Garry doesn't want everybody to know. Why did that story take off? It wasn't even that interesting."

"Because it's timely and people are starting to realize it's common. I suppose it's not so much it was good or interesting, though it was, but that it was right."

She told her grandmother about Jessie in PEI and her brother. And about her friend Julia and her battle.

"Nan, everybody knows somebody with an illness like this, or they struggle themselves. I never had any judgment towards Garry because of his past illness."

"But he feels it you see, he feels judgment, and he fears it, that's why he's angry at you. I'm sure you two will make up again when you get here."

"I don't know Nan, I hope so." But she had a feeling Garry would not forgive her and she wasn't sure she was up to dealing with an angry man even if the anger was deserved.

She pushed along. The landscape of her native land flew past her in a blur, her thoughts elsewhere as she headed home. It wasn't until she pulled in line behind the trail of cars waiting for the last trip to Change Islands she began to feel better. She drove off the ferry twenty minutes later and straight to her Grandmother's old house. Located on the south side, its view of the narrow tickle slowed her heart rate and settled her mind. A feed of Nan's pan-fried cod with rhubarb relish for the potatoes, helped almost as much as her warm embrace and soothing voice.

Charley was home, not in the way she planned but she was here. And though she would prefer to end things with Garry on a friendly note, it had been doomed to end at some point. So, worse-case scenario, she had done what she had set out to do, had an adventure across the country and become a little less ordinary. The number of calls on her phone and messages in her email told her she had become a hell of a lot less ordinary, in fact. She wished somehow, she hadn't destroyed a nice friendship, in the transition.

Chapter 35

No point looking for him honey." Orla Andrews noticed her grand daughter staring at the house next door through the large windows that looked towards Fogo but gave a clear view of Ger's rehabilitated saltbox.

"I wasn't—okay, I admit it, I was. Nan, I can't believe I haven't seen him. I wanted to apologize if I did." She had walked the Squid Jiggers Trail, Shoreline Trail, Indian Lookout Trail, visited the Newfoundland Pony Sanctuary, been in every store, explored the Interpretation Center, took hundreds of pictures and had allowed herself to become enveloped in the peace of her Grandmother's hometown where she had spent the best days of her childhood. There was no sign of Garry anywhere.

"He went on the ferry with Ger this morning, they went to St. John's. They're gone for a week and we'll be on our way before they come back."

"Well crap," her eyes filled. She turned back to the window. "We're going out in boat?" she asked, changing the subject.

"I know you had feelings for him, beyond the regular, friendly kind. Me and Ger were kind of thinking you might like each other."

"We were getting close, yeah." She couldn't discuss this with her grandmother.

"Yes, we're going in boat," she answered the question before Charley could ask a second time.

"Okay good, I better get changed." Charley headed into the bedroom, the little pile of clothes her grandmother had taken off the line, folded and ready for her. She put on a warm sweater determined to enjoy herself despite her disappointment.

Orla Andrews handled a boat as well as any man, having fished for years with her husband before his passing two decades earlier. She lived in Lewisporte in the winter now, in a tiny seniors' cottage. That's where she had first reunited with her old friend Geraldine and her husband, many years before. They purchased the place next door from her as a summer getaway. Originally Orla had rented it to tourists but she decided to let it go to her old friend.

Geraldine's husband had passed but she had kept the place, so now the two women spent summers there, neighbours and best friends again, the decades they had spent apart dissipating like the mist over a grey tickle on a foggy island morning.

Orla kept her boat in excellent condition. And in the summer, she still used it to take advantage of the recreational cod fishery and to sport around a bit in it. They bobbed off towards the west in the direction of Twillingate for a cruise looking for whales and absorbing the bright August day.

Charley found it difficult to enjoy herself though. The only time she managed to forget about the situation with Garry was when she they encountered three Humpbacks "bubble hunting" caplin off the tickle, on their way back.

The large mammals dived and swam, corralling their food, confusing it before they could eat. They surfaced every few minutes and the boat steamed close, the juvenile of the group a tad curious, swimming mere meters from the bow allowing Charley to get amazing shots. Their underwater time became longer and longer, their surfacing further away, one meal ended and the search for the next underway.

"That was incredible. I'm going to put these into an album and do my last Facebook Live from your place, and call this entire trip over."

"I know you want to stop, shut it down but I think you should keep broadcasting. You have a big audience now. You should use that, create awareness about important issues. Have you talked to the CBC yet?" Reporters had been calling for interviews since her arrival.

"Yes, I talked to all of them. I told them I'm doing one final broadcast. Nan, the page has so many followers it's crazy. I called my friend out west to moderate it because there were some negative comments and we've got it under control, but I don't know, I didn't expect it to be like this."

"I know you're feeling bad about Garry, you're going to have to set that right but meanwhile you have a gift. You've always had gifts. You had been headed towards a bright career, you were bound for this. I think you need to think long and hard before you stop."

"I'm not sure the school will think it's okay. It's kind of political. I used my shortened name Charley to hide my identity but I bet like with Garry, they'll figure out I'm Charlotte Andrews." Plus, she would tell them either way because it was fair to do so.

"I'm going to say something now, and it might make you mad," Orla said. They floated along, the late afternoon sun still high behind them, a pale pink and lavender ribbon forming along the westward sky, stretching over the horizon, a sign of the glorious red and gold sunset to come in a few hours. She kept the engine cut so they could talk.

"What?"

"You were anxious to bring attention to Garry's situation or the situation of men like him and you used his personal story. I know, don't say it, you thought it was anonymous, well it wasn't and you used it. I happen to think it had a positive effect because people are talking and when a thousand people talk, one will act and where a hundred-thousand people talk a thousand act. But, well, have you thought about talking of yourself. About what happened to you? You used Garry's story but you've not used your own."

"I can't, Nan." Charley looked down into the bottom of the boat, then off towards the distant shore. The fear of being seen as a victim was almost as great as that of being thought guilty. She wasn't sure why that was, yet.

"I understand, but you should think about it. And perhaps you should think about how if the situations were reversed, and Garry had outed your story, accidental or otherwise, what he would have to do to fix it. Then do that. Not because it'll salvage the friendship or relationship, but because it's the right thing to do. I don't care how difficult your life has been in the past, sometimes you have to suck it up and do the right thing."

It was quite the speech, punctuated by her seventy-five-year-old grandmother hauling the cord on the old Mercury engine with gusto, its sudden whir preventing any possible response.

After docking, Charley hugged her grandmother.

"Thanks Nan. I've got some thinking to do. You gave me a perspective I didn't have before."

"I was thinking you were going to gnaw my head off. Look, don't be hard on yourself. You're a good person, you have a lot to offer and I know you'll do the right thing. I've got to get this boat upon the slip before we leave. I've got a few of the men coming to haul her up. We're chewing up daylight here. I'll be up the once."

Charley made her way into the large kitchen, poured herself a glass of milk and buttered a couple Purity Lemon Cream Crackers. Why was she always hungry here? Perhaps because the air was flavoured with salt.

She looked at the iPad, and pondered her next broadcast. Was she brave enough to do what she knew she must. She jumped when her grandmother's phone rang and answered it, expecting it to be from one of the men who had offered to haul in the boat.

It wasn't, it was Geraldine Clarke, Garry's grandmother.

"Hi Mrs. Clarke," Charlotte said when she recognized her voice.

"Charlotte, my love, and, how are you? Are you having a good visit with Nan?"

"Yes, she's hauling up the yacht now." That was what they jokingly called the eighteen-foot speed boat.

"Getting ready for the trip back?"

"Yeah, we are."

"That's good, will you tell her I called, my love?"

"Ger, how's Garry doing? Is he still mad at me?" She couldn't hang up without asking.

"He 'aven't said much, we have been on the go, he wanted to see the sights. I know he was angry and I can see his point."

"I can too, I don't even know what I was thinking. You know, Ger, I have had a lot of problems, lots of people nosing into my business when I lived here in the province, lived with the judgment and I would never do that to people. I was too confident in the anonymity of it. I guess I didn't realize how fast this thing could take off, I was, quite frankly, stupid. But I'm not a person who would hurt him deliberately. Can you do me a favour?"

"Anything you wants, you knows that." And she meant it. This girl was a sweetheart, she had done amazing things, her broadcasts were funny and smart and had shone a light on some issues and it had been fun to watch her coast from place to place, talking about the country.

"Tell him I'm sorry and I'm going to make it up to him somehow. I don't know how quite yet but I'm going to. And tell him, if he's ever out in BC again, I would love to see him." Her voice broke then because she knew, odds were she would never see him again. But just in case.

"I will tell him all that. And I think he knows , you know, he was just hurt. And scared. He's had a rough go of it."

"Does he seem," she hesitated, afraid of the answer, "depressed?"

"I don't think so, not like he was when he was sick. I think this is normal mad, not the depression he had before."

"I hope not." But she knew depression could be triggered by stress, by emotional events. She hoped he was far enough along in his healing for this not to be the thing to cause a relapse.

"He's laying low, it'll blow over, nobody recognizes him here in town and I think that makes him feel better."

"Good. I'm ending the broadcasts after this one and shutting down the page. Tell him that too."

"Are you sure that's a good idea? You are doing good things."

"But at what cost?"

"Well, I loved it and so did a lot of people but it's your choice, I'll tell Garry what you said."

"Thanks Ger." She hung up and wrote a quick note to her grandmother to tell her that Ger had called, then made her way back to her bedroom, grabbing a notepad to write some ideas for the last broadcast before she left in two days. Her pen scratched along the pages, but nothing came. She looked out at the cluster of men and woman, pulling the boat up the slipway using an old block and tackle pulley system. They all pulled together, on the one rope, their strength multiplied by the simple system and from doing it together.

She started to write again, this time she didn't stop, didn't hesitate, working until her grandmother called her for supper a few hours later, a shift in her mood evident. She tucked into the giant plate of fisherman's brewis after sprinkling sugar liberally over the top and adding some fried pork fat, the sizzling scruncheons drizzled over the mound on her plate.

"Mmmm, Nan, that box of salt cod you packed up better have some hard bread in it."

"Well you're sounding better, you had a nice nap?"

"I was writing, getting ready for tomorrow's broadcast."

"Are you still determined it's going to be the last one?"

"It will all depend on how it goes, Nan, that's all I can say right now." She shoveled another forkful of the delicious fare into her mouth.

Chapter 36

Charley sat on the hill above her grandmother's house, checking the signal. It was strong enough to do the job. The wind had finally dropped so she could tuck away in the "lun", as Nan called it, and not sound like she was in a wind tunnel. The bonus was that the broad expanse of a still, blue ocean was behind her. She tapped the live button, at 7pm as she had posted on the page. People must have been waiting as she was at a thousand views by the time she finished her intro.

"It's Charley here again, checking in from the *Charley Does Canada* tour! How are you all doing? It looks like a lot of you have already connected, why don't you send me a little heart to let me know you're here." She smiled at the little hearts that blipped across the screen, some thumbs-up and of course the usual angry faces. There were haters everywhere on the internet.

"I was pleased to read all of your messages this week. I wanted to do a live stream earlier but my Grandmother's service was slow so it took a few days to get it upgraded to the faster package. So far, it is working well. How's it look? Send me your comments on the quality if you can.

As you can see I'm reporting from a gorgeous spot, that's the Atlantic Ocean behind me, yesterday we took my Grandmother's boat out, saw three humpback whales feeding. As you know I've now been ocean to ocean, and I've driven clear across the country and I thought this would be the time to sum things up.

What have I learned about Canada on this trip? Well, I've learned this country is friggin' massive, the people are amazing, that there are problems but we seem to still have a handle on ourselves, that we sometimes forget the rest of the world doesn't have even half of what we do but we still step up when we're reminded. We have a strong democracy but we need to pay a bit more attention to it. A lot of us are doing wonderful things in our communities, raising wonderful families, welcoming strangers.

I also thought I'd take this opportunity to get more personal. Bear with me, this isn't easy and I'm going to talk about things I've never talked about before. You see, I started my journey and the broadcast of *Charley Through Canada* because I was feeling like I was not living my life to its potential. Don't get me wrong, I have a great life, I live in a gorgeous place, in British Columbia, with a second home in an equally gorgeous place right here. And I have the best country in the world in between them. I'm a privileged person. So, I thought, get out, take a trip, journal it, cover some fun things, highlight some serious things, do something for the greater good, even if it was just to provide a bit of insight and information.

But I've learned something about myself in all of this. As I drove through Canada I discovered this wasn't enough. That I was not being completely honest with you all. Because I'm presenting this person who is together, having fun, all confidence and cockiness and meanwhile I'm this terrified person, setting out under false pretenses. I've given you my first name only but I should have told you my full name is Charlotte Andrews. I've said I'm from British Columbia but I should have said, I live on Bowen Island and teach at the school there. I also should have told you that this past decade and a half it's not so much that I've been living there but that I've been hiding out there. The truth is opposite what you think though. I've discovered that Charley is the real me, Charlotte has been a facade, a surface character. I've not made friends out there, not because people aren't friendly but because I was afraid to get close, I've not dated, not participated in anything social and there is a valid reason for that, which I'm going to share with you right now."

Charley took a deep breath and noted there were over two thousand people watching her broadcast, the little hearts and thumbs crossing the screen in bunches, giving her strength.

"I grew up near here, I spent my summers with Nan, on this island, as sheltered as a girl ever could be. Then went off to university. I was an overachiever, with top marks, I loved life, I loved school, I had a ton of friends. Then I met a man. He was a high school teacher who swept me off my feet and I abandoned my plans and decided to become a teacher too. I fell in love. I didn't see him for what he was though, I was too blinded by what I wanted him to be."

Another big breath.

"The first time he hit me he knocked me unconscious. I came to in the emergency room and he was telling the doctors how I had slipped and fallen. I didn't correct it, thought perhaps I was remembering it wrong. I had a concussion after all. But unfortunately, I wasn't. But I wanted to be so bad. So, I went home with him. And you know how this story is going to go."

A sob caught in her throat, her thoughts firmly in the past now, reliving her horrors, reliving the pain.

"I endured brutality at his hands that changed me forever. I was sexually assaulted and I was beaten. Those who tried to get me out were always so shocked when I went back. But I was too terrified to leave. One time when I did he found me, strangled me until I blacked out. He didn't take me to the hospital, he waited until I came to, then told me to pack or he would do it again. I knew I wouldn't survive the next time. And so, I went back. Time and again. I couldn't leave. I wanted to, but I couldn't. I thank God, every day, I didn't have children. In time I stopped asking for help because I knew people were tired of helping me when I wasn't helping myself. I can't blame them.

Then my escape came but it was at a huge cost. He was arrested for assaulting a student. Some of you will remember the story. We were living in a small town at the time and everybody knew. Some of his friends, teachers even, trashed the girl. Others trashed me. Because I should have known, and stopped it. I can't even begin to tell you how awful my life was then. So, I'll tell you instead that I escaped, moved west, went back to school and became qualified to teach in British Columbia. Then I put my head down and any thoughts of being more than a survivor were banished. I'm telling you this for a few reasons. One, please don't judge those who are going back after abuse. The reasons are complex.

A second one, and this is crucial and something I've learned through my journey back to myself. Domestic and intimate partner abuse isn't a women's problem, it's a men's problem. The women are the victims of this and it creates problems for them, but this is a problem with the men and that's the approach we should take. Men, stop hitting women, stop raping them, stop abusing them, stop threatening them."

She wondered briefly if she was losing people with her rant but she didn't care. She had stuff to say.

"Now I know what comes next. Somebody is going to say, *not all men are like that"* and well duh, of course not. But the ones who are not aren't fixing it either. Go fix your friends, speak up, tell them you disapprove. Do it every time a man puts down a woman in any way. Look there's a lot I can say to all of you, and I can't address the nuances of this problem but I can say that recently I met a man who does stand up. I treasure him dearly. He is kind, patient and has a special strength that is rare. He knows who he is and I'd like to say here how much I respect him and care about him. Even if he never hears it.

I also have a story for you. Earlier today I watched my grandmother haul up her boat. My grandparents fished together for years. There she was with men and women, more men but anyway, it was fun, she was having a laugh with them, it was so healthy and comfortable. They hauled the boat up using what's called a block and tackle system whereby they hook up the boat and the ropes and a set of pulleys multiply the total strength of all the pullers.

Well, there they were, men and women, pulling together, a simple system in place to increase the strength of all of them. And I thought, that's how it's supposed to be, we find the simplest way forward and work together, men and women, to get the job done.

If we can find a way to work on this issue as one, the men taking care of the men's problem, so women feel safe working with them, we can make intimate partner violence and violence against women a rare thing. But it won't happen until a woman is as valued as a human being, as a man is. And it's not going to happen tomorrow but it *can* happen.

One more thing, then I promise I'll shut up. I called this whole endeavor *Charley through Canada*, and the title was intended to be more about the trip, the geographic travel from one coast to the other but it's turned into me discovering Charley, and who she is, what she is and even more importantly where she's headed, *through Canada*. This journey was remarkable because of the places I've seen but more importantly because of the people I've met, from Patsy in Saskatoon, to Brad in Winnipeg, to Christie in Stratford, but most of all because of my favourite Mountie, the kindest, bravest man I've ever known, and because I've already opened my big mouth and let the country know his name, I'll say it here out loud. Garry, they say a Mountie always gets his man. I'm not sure if that's a fact, though I do believe you were a helluva cop, but you sure got my heart. I'll miss you and if you ever find your way to Bowen Island, my address is—"

She paused for a moment then carried on with a grin,.

"Yeah, like I'm telling all of you. Garry, get it from Nan if you ever want it. Thanks Canada. I love you, every single grain of sand, every rock and pebble, every drop of water in your oceans. Hell, I even love the conservatives today. I may as well admit it. Goodbye fellow citizens, until we meet again, Charley, the real Charley, of *Charley Through Canada*, signing off."

Chapter 37

The lazy evening sun sent broad strokes across the hardwood floors of the living room. A small, grey tabby was sprawled in the heat of one of them, stretched out lengthwise so his scrawny body captured as much of the evening heat as it could absorb. The three women were settled into the living room, in their pajamas for a night of Netflix and junk food.

"I've never done this kind of thing before." Charley poured more wine into everybody's glass, draining the last red drop into her own.

"I can't say as I have either," Orla said, admiring the toenails on her right foot while Julia put the finishing touches on the left.

"What? No girl's night? No sitting around, bashing men, eating crap and being female after one of the group has a bad break up? You poor things."

"Well I got married to my first boyfriend and was married until he died. No boyfriends since that and not likely to be one." Orla's face flickered pain at the memory of her only love.

"And I fled and hid, and swore off men forever," Charley said, her eyes drifting to the little red-headed doll sitting on a table between her plants. She had found it in the car when she packed her luggage for the drive back through the country.

"And I've broken up or been dumped so many times it's a ritual," Julia admitted.

"But Mark is working out fairly well?" Charley referred to a new guy Julia was dating.

"He's a nice guy. He has kids though, which is a strange thing for me to think about but I'm taking it one day at a time. I'm not sure he's worthy." She screwed the cap on the top coat bottle and blew a gentle breeze over Orla's toes.

"I'm glad for you," Charley said. She was but she knew a wistful tone had crept into her voice and Julia caught it.

"Do it, spit it out. Purge, tell us how you feel. We're all here for you girlfriend." She moved to sit beside the newly pedicured Orla and slung an arm around her in show of camaraderie."

"I'm not much for spilling my feelings." She wasn't. It felt weak to her and stuffing them was easier.

"You loved the guy and you screwed up," Julia prompted.

"I don't know that it was love."

"Go on, it was, I loved your Grandfather the moment I laid on him, you had several weeks in a car, got to know the guy well and you had plenty of time to fall in love." Orla indicated her wine glass and Julia jumped up to open a second bottle, grabbing a handful of chips along the way.

"I don't know, I mean, I don't know what I feel. I liked him. A lot. Sometimes he had such insight into things, but he was also a bit of a project. Mental health issues and stuff but then I'm a bit of a project too. And what if we had gotten together and he got sick again or worse, I mean, I don't think I could handle that."

"I lost your grandfather and Lord knows he was a project. All savage for the water and the woods, nar bit of time for much else. Dinner on the table at six or he'd be all sooky in front of *Here and Now*. He never said I love you more than once or twice but he was steady and good and funny and smart and I wouldn't trade a second of time with him, to avoid the bit of bad. So long as he is not like the last feller."

"He's nothing like Rick. And I know Nan, I'm trying to pretend I'm not as sad as I am."

"That's some major insight right there?" Julia came back with an open bottle of Merlot and filled Orla's glass. She topped up her own and Charley's and sat down again.

"You going to cry? You're supposed to cry."

"I've already done enough of that. No, it's over, no point rehashing this. I don't want to be pathetic about it. I screwed up royally. I've tried to fix it, yeah, I developed feelings but I'm not sure this is about losing somebody I cared about or the guilt of being the one who caused him pain. Maybe it's both but I'm not going to whine about this all night. Sorry Julia."

"Nah, that's fine. You're right. He's not worth it."

"It's not that he's not worth it Julia. It's that he's worth more than this." She spread her arms in an all-encompassing way.

"What do you mean?"

"I mean he's a real person with real issues. He isn't a *thing* I lost that I should be trivializing. This feels all wrong to me and I know it's how you cope with breakups but it's not me. I don't want to hurt your feelings but what works for you, isn't working for me, it feels contrived and immature."

She sobbed, then realized her speech may have offended the only friend she had.

"Oh God, I didn't mean that what you do is trivial or immature, this isn't coming out right, don't stop being my friend though okay?" she pleaded. Charley drained her wine glass then turned to hide tears that formed during her passionate speech.

"Stop being your friend? Sure, you're the best person I've met since I've been here. I know we've only started getting close recently but all my real-good friends are off the island and so having you here has been great. And it *is* contrived and immature but that's because rituals make me happy. They're like prayers without the dogma. Makes me feel connected to the sisterhood. You know, bullshit like that." Julia looked straight at Charley.

"Okay, good." Charley wiped away the tears that filled her eyes and rolled down her cheeks. She needed a friend more than ever now.

"But if you want me to punch a man for you, I will okay?"

They laughed, but Orla didn't.

"I never knew you were so alone out here." Orla's eyes were full, her granddaughter's sadness her own.

"I wasn't. I thought I wasn't. I never walked around feeling unhappy but something woke up in me on the trip, having a companion the entire time, having somebody to talk to about things, to learn from, to be with. Maybe that's what Garry was more than anything, a friend. I needed a friend and I didn't even know I did."

"You lost all your friends those years you were married."

"I could have gotten some of them back but I ran away."

"And many more were awful to you, no wonder you didn't want people around."

"We're all damaged, aren't we? Fucked up. Oh, Sorry Orla," Julia apologized.

"Don't worry about saying fuck around me," Orla laughed," I'm where Charley learned her language skills."

"I have another ritual, I really want to do this one," Julia pleaded. It was silly and fun but something she liked to do when somebody needed to get over something.

"Oh, I'll humour you. Go ahead."

Julia pulled out a large powder brush.

"Lie back and I'll start."

Charley laid back in the chair and closed her eyes like Julia indicated. The brush touched her cheek, the fibers tickling as it moved from the center of forehead between her eyes in an outward motion, going around and around from that point.

"Relax and release, let me paint magic into your life, let me brush away all that is negative and sad, all that is hurtful and unsatisfying, let me paint magic."

Charley drifted away under her ministrations, enjoying the brush feather across her skin over and over as Julia repeated her words. Her entire body relaxed, her mind drifting across the expanse of the country from the white snows at the tips of the Rockies, to the golden waving wheat of

Saskatchewan and further to the great green fields of rural Ontario. She saw the drifts of pure white that filled the land in places she had never been and in winters yet to return. Her mind drifted to the book-end blues of the oceans and into the depths of the dark eyes of a certain Mountie who had held her hand as they crossed the land, two explorers out to discover a country only to find themselves and each other. She felt the air around her change as she relaxed into the realization that even if she never saw him again he had painted some magic into her life, had given it colour, and that as they had driven through Canada he had allowed her to see the blemishes in the land as well as the beauty. And he hadn't painted over them, he had highlighted them, for they were as valid as any of the pretty parts. They were the signs of the wrongs of the past and the indicators of where the work needed to be done. Both in the country, and in herself.

Julia's brush strokes slowed until they came to a stop and Charley opened her eyes, a smile across her features, a new light in her eyes as she sat up, as relaxed as she had ever been in her life.

"Wow, that was amazing, what did you do?"

"I painted magic," she said, "Orla, your turn."

And as Orla submitted to the gentle brush strokes Charley smiled. She knew what she would do and how she would go on with her life. She'd paint some magic of her own, make some gentle strokes, do what needed to be done to heal some of the problems. She sipped her wine as her grandmother drifted into a soft snooze.

From now on she would do better, be more. She had a platform and could influence people, could do so much better than before. She had become a better Charley, now it was time she became a better citizen.

Chapter 38

Charley hadn't been this nervous about the upcoming first day of school since her mom had taken her tiny hand and led her to Miss Bursey's kindergarten class when she was five years old. She had kept her life so closed off from her work she had no idea how her friends and staff would respond now that the word of her big tour was common knowledge. The people she ran into thought it was great but the administration, well she would see in two short days if it impacted her job in any way.

Now that she had every single detail organized for her first day back she was ready to take Julia up on her offer to have drinks outside. Like every year, the rain on the day she had left the island had been one of the few rainy days of the summer. The rest of the season remained hot and dry, with no precipitation in the immediate forecast.

Charley knew though, in October the rain would come. And stay. So, she spent as much time as possible outside, recruiting Julia as a hiking buddy, the two of them becoming closer and closer as they trekked up hills and stared out over panoramic views. Orla had stayed a week, hopping on a plane and getting out of there, to do a bit of fall fishing. Those caught in the fall were the best cod for splitting and salting after all.

Garry still crossed Charley's mind off and on, all day long. She regretted the missed opportunity though she had found new direction, started volunteering and giving her blog a more activist bend. People wanted the fun and happy version of the country but she added in some of the things that needed work. There was a backlash, she lost some readers but she gained more. Interesting things were happening including a call from a publishing company.

She emailed Garry as soon as she was asked to write *Charley Through Canada*, the book. She could write it without him. But she wanted his permission. She even hoped he might help her write it. So far there was no response.

But that wasn't all she missed. There had been a connection between them and she had messed it up. She knew they could have made it as a couple. She loved him. It was that simple. It wasn't the obsessive, unnatural, blind love she had experienced with Rick, but rather it was an open-hearted feeling based upon mutual respect, understanding, cemented in the knowledge he was a decent man. Sure, they had geography against them but they could have used Skype and text and the plain old telephone and gotten to know each other even better until they were sure. Perhaps he didn't share the feelings she had for him, not anymore , since she had let him down. But before that, yeah, there had been a chance. She'd blown it.

The house phone rang. Charley jumped. Nan was the only one who used it so she answered with a happy hello.

"Hi Charley, it's Garry," he cleared his throat, "I got your email, and well, if you want to write the book go ahead."

Charley's head spun. Garry. What the hell?

"How did you know this number? Not that I care you called it, I mean I'm glad you called, happy you called. About the book. It's good to hear from you." She was breathless. She was rambling. She put her hand over the mouthpiece, took a deep breath and walked towards the couch. Be calm, don't blow this, she told herself.

She knocked over a plant, dirt flying in every direction and from the couch cushion the tabby kitten arched its back and hissed at the sudden noise.

"Shhhh, Hans Solo." She made her way to him, stepping on the dirt, tracking it across the floor. So much for calm.

"What? What happened? Are you okay?"

"Fine, I knocked a plant over, the kitten is upset, it's nothing,"

"You adopted a kitten?"

"Yeah, his name is Han Solo. He's eight weeks old." She petted the fluffy feline who settled down on her lap, quiet purrs calming Charley's heart.

"Great name. So, yeah, I got your number from Orla, you said it was okay."

"Why not call my cell phone? You already had that number."

"I was so angry I deleted it," he admitted, "also, your grandmother said, this is the phone to call you at to get you at home."

"I guess Nan thinks that because it's the number she always uses." Wow, he had deleted her number, he was that pissed.

"Yeah, I guess so. So , that's why I called. To let you know you can write the book. But I'd like to help and have some say in what is in there."

Charley took a deep breath.

"Garry, I'm sorry. I didn't think, I mean, I got carried away in trying to do something good, I broke a confidence and I shouldn't have. That was your story to tell. I will do the book with you, either way, but I need to know you forgive me. And that you know I'll never do anything like that again."

"Charley, forget about it. I forgive you. I was pissed, I admit. My grandmother was worried about me falling back into depression but the anger was at least a feeling so I didn't. Well, not until the anger went away, and we were home and you were gone."

"Thank you, I—" but he interrupted before she could go on.

"But I picked up the phone a lot to call you. And put it back down. I didn't know what to say. I was almost ready to call finally and then your email came, and it was about more publicity, more of my story being out there. I lost my nerve again. I'm just now getting it back."

"We don't have to do the book you know. I've had some calls from women's advocacy groups asking me to speak. I'd like to do more of that," she rushed. She needed him to know didn't care a speck about the damned book or anything else except he forgive her.

"You should do it, I've had a similar experience. I've had some calls too, I was interviewed here by CBC and well, I got a lot of positive feedback from people who have been through what I've been through. Often men who have tried to, well, you know. And people who love men who have succeeded. I realized I had been harbouring a fear of the stigma so long I forgot hiding was not helping, so I think maybe we can both work on our causes, help others, and heal a bit."

"Wow. Garry, that is great. I want to tell you that the trip, with you, it changed my life. I think if I had taken it alone it would have been okay but you added something. You were an amazing friend to me, you made me safe, you helped me trust. That first night, in the Hostel, I did not sleep at all."

"I know. I didn't either. I heard you moving around and I knew you had gone through some stuff. I didn't know what but I was on alert in case you needed me. I had to pee around 5am but didn't get up to go because I was afraid I'd frighten you."

"I didn't get up until 7am. You held it two hours?"

"I nearly burst. But I didn't and you did trust me after."

"I still do Garry. I just wish—"

"What?"

"That we could have stayed together, worked on the book together. I had thought of asking you to drive back with me, before I blew it all to bits. To see, I don't know, you seemed to be ready for more and I thought maybe we could have been together, or even get to know each other, maybe you could come back out if we found out we wanted that…I'm rambling here but I know, it's too late for that…but if we could be friends?"

"Well I guess we'll never know now, will we?"

"No, I guess not."

"Okay well, get in touch with me about the book." Damn, she had scared him off, his voice had drifted away. Perhaps he had never wanted more than friendship so now he was uncomfortable. Double Damn.

"I will. Thanks."

"Good bye, see you soon." Charley held the silent telephone receiver to her ear a while longer. The kitten on her lap shifted a bit as she set it down on the arm of the couch.

"I am doomed to be the lonely crazy cat lady Han Solo."

The cat jumped up, leapt off her lap and fled to the kitchen.

"Or not." She glared at the mess. Well there had been a reconciliation, some forgiveness, a book would get written and maybe in time they would get close again. Meanwhile she had to clean up the dirt on her living room floor and water her plants.

The End

(just kidding, turn the page)

Chapter 39

The doorbell rang a few moments later and Charley yelled to Julia, who intended to stop by, to come on in. She needed to talk to her now. Try to sort through the conversation with Garry. When she didn't enter right away Charley gave an exasperated gasp and set down her watering pitcher to go answer it. She opened the door to a delivery person who stood there with the largest flower arrangement she had ever seen.

"Oh, my God they're beautiful," she said. Leaving the poor guy standing there, she ruffled through the large sprigs of greenery and the bright fragrant blossoms for a clue as to who had sent it. She hadn't received flowers in a long time. Perhaps they were from one of her fans. She did have some.

"Is there a card?" she asked the man, whose face was masked by the enormous bouquet.

"No, there isn't but I have a message for you from the sender."

Charley's eyes widened, her lips formed a little O as he handed her the arrangement. She still didn't take it from him, too shocked when she saw his face.

"Garry," Charley stepped back, "what the fuck are you doing here?"

"I said I'd see you soon. I couldn't let this all end like a Canadian movie now, could I? Leave things hanging?" His eyes flashed and a grin broke on his face.

"You arse! How the hell did you get here?" She laughed at his joke all the same.

"I flew." He waited for that to sink in.

"You flew? Wow, you did it? Here, give me those." She finally grabbed the flowers and set them on the table by the door, and turned back to him.

"Yep, I flew. I wanted to see you."

"You Jackass, I thought when you dismissed me on the phone right then—you're mean."

"Orla said you would call me that for surprising you but insisted I come anyway."

"My grandmother told you to come? Come in, sit down, here, there is dirt in the living room." She led him to the kitchen, opening the fridge. Getting them a beer each, she twisted the top of them, took a swig of hers and put one on the island for Garry.

"Your grandmother, my grandmother, everybody who I've talked to in the past couple of weeks. They thought we should end up together, like a couple."

"You got on a plane, traveled all the way across the country? Garry, that's huge, I'm proud of you. That was truly brave." Her eyes filled with tears at the thought of him doing that. Also, a couple? Her heart got a bit pitty-patty and her belly flip-flopped. Was she friggin' twelve?

"I did, two planes. And it was fine. I don't know, the fear is gone. I was anxious but felt like I could control it. It's always going to be a battle but I figured if I freaked out and the plane had to land, well, then the plane had to land. If I was on it and somebody had a heart-attack I'd be understanding. So why not be understanding of my own illness?"

"Gobsmacked."

"Me too," Garry grinned, "or as they say now, I'm woke." He did what was supposed to be some cool gesture to accompany his proclamation of woke-ness.

"I'm glad you're here. You can't pull that off by the way. "She mimicked his gesture.

"Damn, but I feel woke anyway, I'm looking at a small apartment a few blocks from here, I don't expect you to let me live here but I do want to spend time with you, see if we're going anywhere. I'm in no rush, but I want to work on the book with you, hike, date, see where things go. What do you think?"

"So, um, you're staying?" This was even better, she was expecting it was a vacation. He wasn't going back. She would never let him go back.

"Only if you think I should."

"I most definitely think you should." She moved closer then, put her arms around his neck and reach up for his lips, but barely had they met when a little tabby ball of fur leaped upon the kitchen island, ran towards them, climbed on Garry's shoulder, and licked his face.

"What the hell?"

"Han Solo, this is Indiana Jones, Indiana Jones, Han Solo."

"You're nuts," Garry grinned, stroking the tiny kitten who snuggled against him, rubbing his fur against his face.

"He owns you now, they told me at the rescue they rub against you because they're claiming you."

"Really, well then—" he put the tiny feline down and moved closer to Charley, rubbing himself against her. She laughed then moved her head, rubbing it against his chest.

"Are you claiming my heart?" he asked.

"Yes," she replied then gave a resounding hoot, "that's the corniest fucking thing I've ever done or said in my god-damned life."

"Me too," he agreed, going in for a kiss while the grey tabby bounded off to tip-toe through the dirt on the living room floor.

***

"Ready Indiana Jones?"

"Yes boss." Garry fixed his baseball hat and adjusted his glasses. Charley clicked the button, and they were live on Facebook a short time later.

"Hello everybody, it's me again, Charley Andrews and I'm thrilled to be back, this time because I have my partner from *Charley through Canada* with me. I finally coerced him with cheap beer and cold hard Canadian cash to do this. Be kind to him, he's a virgin of Facebook live. But he needed to be here to help me out, because he's the co-author of the book, released today, in both official languages, and appropriately named, *Charley Through Canada*, so without further ado, Canada, meet Garrison Ford Clarke."

"Hi Canadians, it's a pleasure to be here and please, it's just Garry, and for the record I'm completely pissed that it's not *Charley and Garry Through Canada*, so unfair," he shook his head in mock disbelief.

"Oh puh-lease! You were a hitch-hiker, a bit player, the stowaway, I was the main character." She grinned at him.

"You're a character, I'll give you that."

She nudged him with an elbow.

"Well the cat likes me better at least." He continued his banter.

"That's true folks, my cat, who I rescued from certain death, saved all his nine lives," she said, before adding, "off topic but please rescue, spay and neuter your pets, now, where was I?" She looked at Garry for a clue.

"Cat likes me best." he repeated.

"Yeah, the cat I saved actually prefers my co-writer here to me. Can you believe it? He's my first cat and what I've learned about cats is they're unpredictable, maniacal, yet somehow funny and adorable."

"Just like you."

"Shut up Garry. Oh wait, funny and adorable? Yes, and you're cute. So, that's good. Today we're here to tell you about the book that speaks to our adventures and more than that, it will tell you about the things we learned as we made our way by car, through Canada. And to let you know we're going to do a book tour!"

"A tour *through Canada.*" Garry exaggerated the last two words. Charley shot him a glare.

"Well it is. I'm branding, the publisher likes that." He moved forward, staring straight into the camera as he said it.

The several thousand tuning in to the live-stream sent a pile of laugh emoticons. He was a natural.

"Anyway, the book is out, it's available in paperback and on Amazon Kindle, iTunes books and Kobi."

"And Nan's living room, and Charley's grandmother's living room," Garry added.

"Yep, and my living room, and they're all signed by me and Garry here. And it's available in bookstores across the country. Check our page for the tour dates."

"Also, check our page for our causes, donate money or your time to help with the issues near and dear to us, domestic violence prevention and mental health services and aboriginal causes as well. We will be donating all of the proceeds from the book sales evenly to those three through the charities listed," Charley continued.

"Because we're independently wealthy and don't need the money," Garry quipped.

"No because we care about these causes. But we do have enough so it's time to share." She pretended to be annoyed at him.

"So, we're just good folks?" His innocent look was priceless.

"Yes Garry," her faux patient smile was perfect, " like most Canadians Garry, we're just good folks. Now Garry's going to say all of that in French."

Garry repeated it all, sometimes with such an impish grin Charley interrupted to ask what he was saying about her.

"I said you were pretty," he lied after he said, "Je vais lui demander de m'epouser tres bientot."

He did the final thank you in his other language and Charley ended it in English.

"Thank you, Canada for tuning in and I'll straighten Garry out once we end this live stream. See you next time on *Charley Through Canada* when we check in from the tour. Bye for now."

She picked up a pillow and whacked Garry.

"What?" He arranged his face into an innocent look.

"You know what," she advised. But her eyes were happy.

"I do," he admitted, grinning.

"What do you have to say for yourself then?"

"I would like to say," he paused, looked at the computer, "that you forgot to end the live stream." And he started to laugh.

"No friggin' way," she looked at the screen too, then cracked up laughing herself, trying to apologize, unable to speak, she waved at the people watching, trying to catch her breath. She hit the stop button and fell against him, her laughter uncontrollable, holding her stomach.

A sizable grey tabby kitten came flying into the room and insinuated himself between the two humans who would have gone from hysterical laughter to making out without his interference. Instead they calmed themselves down, chuckling on occasion, petting the purring animal.

"You know what Charley Andrews?" Garry said, eyes narrow, smile gentle.

"What?"

"I love you."

"I love you too Garrison Ford Clarke."

"My real name, you used my real name," he jested.

"I didn't want to confuse the cat."

Charley smiled and kissed him on the lips.

The absolute very end.

(But if you don't believe me, turn the page)

It really is the end but if you liked Charley through Canada, you might also enjoy *The Secrets of Rare Moon Tickle* by the same author.

About the Book

In a delicately woven tapestry of the mystic and the earthy, author Carolyn R. Parsons brings you into the lives of Christianna Cormack and Joe Indigo. Spanning nearly two decades, it follows the couple from their first meeting until they are ripped apart by his foolish choices. When Christianna moves to Rare Moon Tickle, Newfoundland and Labrador, she is informed there are no secrets in a small town but she proves this adage wrong when destiny colludes with nature to ensure her inevitable reunion with Joe. Their love is now forbidden and one lie leads to another. As if suspended from cosmic puppet strings, Christianna cannot escape the web of secrecy and though she tries to live a normal, happy life, she discovers fate has other ideas in *The Secrets of Rare Moon Tickle.*

Available in paperback and e-book.

Find Carolyn R. Parsons

website: www.carolynrparsons.webs.com
Twitter: @carolynrparsons
Instagram: @carolynrparsons
Facebook: www.facebook.com/carolynparsonsbooks

I love talking to readers. Please contact me at:

Email: carolynrparsons@gmail.com
Telephone: 709-571-3470

Other Books by Carolyn R. Parsons

Breezedaze; Poetry from the Breeze (Poetry Collection 2009)
The Secrets of Rare Moon Tickle (Novel 2010)

Cover Design by Majeau Designs

https://www.facebook.com/MajeauDesigns/

A publication of Rose Enna Imprints

ABOUT THE AUTHOR

Carolyn R. Parsons is a Canadian writer. Her early background is in business, first in finance and later in a media environment. After she escaped from those two highly entertaining (yawn) fields she started her writing career. She published two books in 2009 and 2010, had poetry printed in numerous anthologies and spent a few years writing newspaper and magazine articles including a bi-weekly arts feature, a weekly column as well as general news stories. An activist, feminist, parent, spouse and cat owner, she spends her free time weaving stories and convincing herself a nap is better for her health than a walk. Her next novel, *Desolate* is being released in 2017, by Rose Enna Imprints. A series of three romance novels will be released this year under the pseudonym CA Rose.